A MIDWINTER'S WEDDING

THE FOUR KINGDOMS AND BEYOND

THE FOUR KINGDOMS

The Princess Companion: A Retelling of The Princess and the Pea
(Book One)

The Princess Fugitive: A Reimagining of Little Red Riding Hood
(Book Two)

The Coronation Ball: A Four Kingdoms Cinderella Novelette

Happily Every Afters: A Reimagining of Snow White and Rose Red
(Novella)

The Princess Pact: A Twist on Rumpelstiltskin (Book Three)

A Midwinter's Wedding: A Retelling of The Frog Prince (Novella)

The Princess Game: A Reimagining of Sleeping Beauty (Book Four)

The Princess Search: A Retelling of The Ugly Duckling (Book Five)

BEYOND THE FOUR KINGDOMS

A Dance of Silver and Shadow: A Retelling of The Twelve Dancing
Princesses (Book One)

A Tale of Beauty and Beast: A Retelling of Beauty and the Beast
(Book Two)

A Crown of Snow and Ice: A Retelling of The Snow Queen (Book Three)

A Dream of Ebony and White: A Retelling of Snow White (Book Four)

A Captive of Wing and Feather: A Retelling of Swan Lake (Book Five)

A Princess of Wind and Wave: A Retelling of The Little Mermaid
(Book Six)

RETURN TO THE FOUR KINGDOMS

A MIDWINTER'S WEDDING

A RETELLING OF THE FROG PRINCE

MELANIE CELLIER

LUMINANT PUBLICATIONS

A MIDWINTER'S WEDDING: A FOUR KINGDOMS NOVELLA

ISBN 978-0-6483051-0-1

Luminant Publications
PO Box 203
Glen Osmond, South Australia 5064

melaniecellier@internode.on.net
http://www.melaniecellier.com

Cover Design by Karri Klawiter

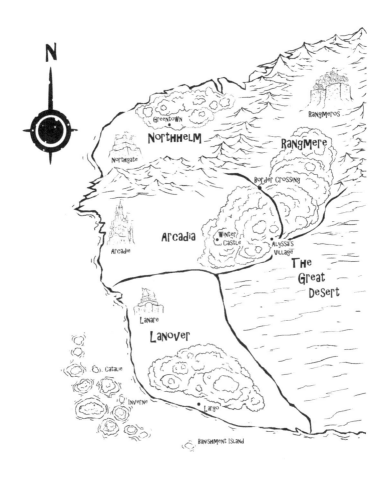

Royal Family of Lanover

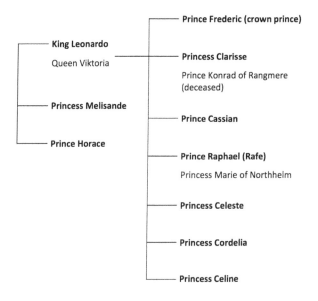

King Leonardo
Queen Viktoria

Prince Frederic (crown prince)

Princess Clarisse
Prince Konrad of Rangmere (deceased)

Princess Melisande

Prince Cassian

Prince Horace

Prince Raphael (Rafe)
Princess Marie of Northhelm

Princess Celeste

Princess Cordelia

Princess Celine

A GIFT

"*I*t's a present."

Princess Cordelia looked down at the golden ball and then up into the stunningly beautiful face of her sister. "Umm, thanks?"

Ever since the curse, Cordelia was used to her sister doing senseless, empty-headed things, but the unexpected gift seemed odd even for her. It wasn't as if it was Cordelia's birthday or anything.

"It's not for you, silly!" Celeste laughed, and the golden, musical sound filled the small garden. Her laugh was almost as irresistible as her face.

If any courtiers had been there, they would have sighed and murmured to each other. Cordelia could easily imagine what they would say. *Such a beautiful girl. Such a pity about the curse.*

She almost sighed herself. Not because of the wasted beauty of her older sister, though. Life as a sixth child had enough challenges of its own. No one noticed you when you were constantly surrounded by the beauty and talents of your older siblings. And Cordelia wasn't even the baby of the family, a position that attracted at least some attention.

She reminded herself, for the thousandth time, that she should be grateful. After all, if she'd been the most beautiful of them all, then she would have been the one with the curse.

But despite the reminder, she couldn't help wishing that, just once, she could stand on her own. That she could meet someone who would see her as Cordelia, rather than as yet another one of that horde up at the palace. Even poor, cursed Celeste had gone on a visit of state to their northern neighbor Arcadia a year and a half ago, when she was Cordelia's age.

Celeste was still smiling, apparently oblivious to Cordelia's discontent. "It's for Princess Marie. As a wedding present. She's marrying our brother Rafe, remember?"

"Of course I remember!" snapped Cordelia and then instantly regretted it. It wasn't Celeste's fault that she was such a fool. She softened her tone. "But I don't know why you're giving it to me."

"Oh! Haven't you heard? The wedding is to be held on Midwinter's Day, which means any attendees will be snowed in for the whole season. Mother and Father have decided they can't be away for that long. But Rafe will be so sad if none of us attend." Her smile grew even brighter. "So they've decided to send you."

"Me?" Cordelia stared at her, hardly able to believe her good fortune. "Only me?"

"That's why I'm giving you the ball. For our new sister."

Cordelia tried to contain her glee. It seemed too good to be true. And Rafe was her favorite brother, too. She bit her lip. She would have to think of an amazing wedding gift for him. She glanced down at the golden ball that her sister had deposited in her hands.

"Is it real gold?" she asked, curiosity momentarily distracting her. "It's very light."

"Of course it's real! Only the best for our dear Rafe." Celeste leaned forward as if imparting a secret. "I think it might be magic. I got it from Godmother. It's supposed to help you find true love."

"Well it doesn't seem to have helped you," pointed out Cordelia.

She didn't mean it harshly. It was just the truth. The three youngest Lanoverian princesses often bemoaned the lack of romance in their lives.

Celeste leaned back and looked puzzled. "No, it hasn't, has it? Maybe it's not magic after all. That might have been a game I was playing... I can't quite remember now." Her words trailed off as she began to hum to herself happily.

Cordelia bit back an impatient retort. Celeste couldn't be held responsible for the foolish things she said. Still, the younger princess couldn't resist asking the obvious question. "Well, if it *is* magic, why would you give it to a bride? She's already found true love."

Celeste stopped humming and leaned forward again. "I've heard rumors of dangerous things afoot in Northhelm. I thought a godmother item might help, and it's the only one I have."

Cordelia considered reminding her sister that Rafe and Marie had already defeated the danger in Northhelm but decided against it. She had far more important things to do—like pack!

But first she would find her mother and make sure Celeste was telling the truth. She ran out of the garden with a light heart.

CHAPTER 1

*C*ordelia bounced once on the seat of the carriage and then subsided after a stern look from her personal maid. She would have made a face except she could hear Celeste's warnings in her mind. Celeste had told her many times that a princess should never make faces since it diminished her beauty. And beauty was the one topic where Celeste's judgment couldn't be questioned.

Cordelia settled for a small sigh instead.

She had been so excited when her mother had confirmed that she would be traveling to Northhelm to attend Rafe's wedding. The emotion had been somewhat dampened, however, when her mother insisted that Priscilla accompany her. As a personal maid, Priscilla left a lot to be desired. As a combination of nanny, governess, and parental substitute, Queen Viktoria thought she was perfect. And nothing Cordelia could say had convinced her mother that she was too old to need a baby-sitter.

She supposed she should be grateful she had been allowed to come at all. Her parents hadn't wanted any of the family to travel so far and be gone for so long. Instead they had dispatched the Duchess of Sessily, along with a large retinue, to support Rafe in the various negotiations and treaties that would surround the wedding. The older woman was a diplomatic genius, and the kingdom had proven safe in her hands many times before.

When their children had questioned the decision, the king and queen had assured them that they would fund a royal tour for the newlyweds to visit Lanover after the wedding. They would all get the chance to meet their new sister.

Except when Rafe heard that the duchess was already on her way without any of his family, he had sent a letter pleading on behalf of his three younger sisters. King Leonardo and Queen Viktoria had decided that, while Celeste had already had her turn in Arcadia and Celine was far too young, Cordelia should be allowed to attend after all.

Celine had complained—that went without saying—but their mother had done nothing but repeat the same placid, unmoving reply. "You're too young." Of course none of the princesses were fooled by this. Celine wasn't too young. She was too wild and too tempestuous.

At least those were the words Priscilla used. Their two oldest brothers used even less complimentary words. And their mother simply sighed and reminded them all that she was still young yet.

Cordelia threw off thoughts of her sisters. The carriage had entered Northgate, the capital of Northhelm, several minutes before, and she wanted to stick her head out the window so she could get a good look at the city. She snuck a glance at Priscilla and then decided against it. The older woman watched her with a hawk-like stare.

She sighed again and contented herself with absorbing as much of the view as she could see from inside the vehicle. Priscilla had been nanny to the older Lanoverian princes and princesses but had handed over the role before Cordelia arrived. Cordelia wished the dour woman had retired instead of staying on in the palace. Even Celeste, who didn't normally worry about much apart from her looks, found Priscilla overly strict.

The city seemed smaller than the Lanoverian capital, and the differences didn't stop there. The warmer southern climate meant Cordelia had grown up in a sprawling, dusty city, composed mostly of single-story buildings made of reddish sandstone. Even her own home, the palace, consisted of only one story.

In contrast, Northgate had quaint cobbled streets lined by tall houses, each connected to the neighboring home to form long unbroken rows of buildings. Their window boxes were empty of flowers due to the season, but the streets were brightened by lanterns on black metal poles.

The sun hadn't set, but the lanterns already glowed, combating the overcast sky. The whole effect was already quaint and picturesque even without the added advantage of softly falling snow.

"Look, Priscilla!" Cordelia couldn't contain her glee. "It's snowing!"

"I have observed, Your Highness."

Cordelia tightened her lips and kept her eyes glued to the window. She refused to let the other woman ruin her enjoyment of the moment. The travelers had pushed themselves for weeks to make it to Northhelm before the winter weather made travel impossible. Cordelia was just glad they were there.

"Ohh…" The soft sound of enchantment slipped unconsciously from her mouth. The palace had come into view, and the tall building of white stone looked even more beautiful than she had imagined.

According to Celeste, the elegant Arcadian palace was even more impressive than this one. But Cordelia was in the mood to be impressed, and she found the Northhelmian palace more than lived up to her expectations.

She was still admiring it when her carriage passed through the gates and pulled to a stop in the front courtyard.

"Stay here," said Priscilla before climbing out and beginning to order about their various guards and grooms, as well as the Northhelmian servants who had come rushing out to help. With four carriages, a great many riders, and even more luggage, the traveling party took some time to disperse.

Cordelia restrained her impatience, occupying herself with her usual game. Staring at the seat in front of her, she formed a mental picture of what was happening outside. She could hear three Northhelmian grooms directing the Lanoverians where to send their horses. Several more servants unloaded the luggage under the direction of both Priscilla and a Northelmian woman, presumably the housekeeper.

She was entertaining herself by imagining the faces that belonged to the voices when another voice caught her ear. The tone marked it as belonging to a noble, and it sounded distant from the melee around the carriage.

Cordelia doubted any of the other Lanoverians could hear it; even she had nearly missed it, and she not only had excellent hearing but was paying close attention. She let the other noises fade away and focused in the direction of the voice.

"So, the first of them arrives." That was a second voice, markedly less noble.

"No, no, that's a Lanoverian royal carriage. And, anyway, the southerners only sent one of the younger princesses." The noble voice sounded impatient.

"Oh." A pause. "Aren't we interested in Lanover then?"

"So far, Lanover appears to have escaped the general madness. Only their third prince has been infected, and he's defected to Northhelm from what we hear."

Cordelia frowned and bit her lip. The voices were speaking about her and Rafe, but the words didn't quite make sense. They did, however, make her feel uneasy. Madness? Defection? What did they mean? She decided to peek out the window and see if she could spy the owners of the voices.

As she began to move toward the far window, the door on the palace side opened.

"Your Highness."

Cordelia froze, half off the seat. She reminded herself that looking out the window wasn't a crime—even in Priscilla's strict rulebook. She had no reason to feel guilty.

Priscilla looked around the interior of the vehicle, as if searching for the source of Cordelia's guilt, and then settled for shaking her head. Stepping back, she gestured for the princess to alight.

Cordelia glanced once more toward the window and then hopped out of the carriage. From an unobstructed view, the palace looked even more impressive. All of its windows were ablaze, and the light shone on the softly falling snow. She forgot momentarily about the strange overheard conversation at the beautiful sight.

Her carriage was already being whisked away by several grooms, and the mountains of luggage they had brought with them had disappeared into the palace. Cordelia looked around, hoping that Rafe might have come to greet her.

As she surveyed the large courtyard, she admitted to herself that she would be happy enough to see anyone. Well, anyone more sympathetic than Priscilla, anyway.

Even as she thought it, a lone rider trotted through the palace gates. He wore a military uniform and rode a beautiful chestnut horse. Cordelia's love for horses gave her a soft spot for anyone who could ride well. And this man had one of the best seats she'd seen in a long time.

He pulled up, facing away from her, and began a conversation with a groom. Cordelia ignored Priscilla, who was motioning for her to proceed inside, and lingered in the courtyard, hoping the rider might dismount and move toward the palace doors.

Sure enough, the newcomer swung down from the saddle and handed his reins to the groom. A little thrill rushed through her body. In truth, she wanted an audience as much as she wanted sympathy.

After all, she was one of the Lanoverian princesses, famed throughout the Four Kingdoms for their great beauty. Every day her mirror told her how lovely she was to look at. Unfortunately, her eyes also told her that she was the least remarkable of her six siblings. What was the point being beautiful if you spent your life standing next to Celeste?

But now her chance had come. Only one of her siblings was in Northhelm with her, and he didn't count. She resisted the urge to pat her hair and straighten her dress, and instead put on a bright smile.

The rider turned and took two steps toward the palace before he looked up and noticed Priscilla and Cordelia. His gaze glanced over the older lady and then settled on the princess.

Cordelia smiled encouragingly.

His look of shocked surprise was familiar—she had seen it often enough on the faces of young men the first time they saw Celeste. How entirely different it felt, though, to have it directed at her.

Except his expression didn't progress to one of admiration. Instead it transformed into a look much more closely resembling distaste. After a frozen moment, he wheeled around and hurried past the side of the palace and out of sight.

Cordelia's smile dropped. She ducked her head and rushed up the palace steps, propelled forward by the heat in her cheeks. Her gut churned with embarrassment, and the warmth from her face seemed to wash over her whole body. Her one relief was that no one but Priscilla had been present to witness her foolishness.

What had she been thinking? A few weeks of travel hadn't made her experienced and sophisticated. She was as unimportant in Northhelm as she had always been in Lanover.

CHAPTER 2

*T*wo steps into the palace, Cordelia collided with someone. Gasping, she tried to step backward but was instead gripped firmly in place.

"Woah there, Dellie," said a familiar voice, and she nearly melted from relief. Rafe.

She looked up, and his laughter changed to concern when he saw her expression.

"Is everything all right?" he asked.

She nodded and then squeaked and buried her face in his chest.

She could picture the bemused shake of his head as he wrapped her in his arms and murmured unintelligible soothing noises. He didn't ask any more questions and Cordelia's sick feeling drained away in his solidly familiar presence. Rafe was a favorite with all three of his younger sisters for a reason.

Cordelia knew that Celeste was his favorite—they were the closest together in age and had been the best of friends before the curse—but in that moment she didn't care. After several more heartbeats, she drew a deep breath and stepped back.

"Feel better now?" he asked, the usual teasing light in his eyes.

"Much," she said, her own smile returning.

A voice next to Rafe chimed in. "What a delightful brother you are! So understanding. William should take lessons."

Rafe laughed while Cordelia took in the tall girl standing next to him.

"Believe me," he said, "with three younger sisters, I long ago gave up on *understanding*. I settle for general sympathy, and it seems to be well received." He puffed out his chest in what was clearly meant to be a joking way. "I'm rather a favorite, you know."

Realizing that the girl must be Princess Marie, Cordelia rushed to back him up. "It's true. Everyone back home loves Rafe."

He grinned. "Well, those who don't think me entirely too frivolous and light-hearted, anyway."

Cordelia waved her hand dismissively. "You're forgetting, Clarisse isn't at home anymore—she lives in Rangmere now."

Rafe snorted and then looked at Marie. "You'll understand when you meet the rest of my siblings. Clarisse is my oldest sister and the one who most disapproves of my frippery self. All of us younger ones like to make fun of how seriously the older ones take everything. I guess it comes from all that responsibility."

Marie raised one eyebrow.

"Not that I'm in any way lacking in responsibility, of course," Rafe hurried to add.

For a brief moment, Cordelia worried that Rafe had gotten himself betrothed to someone who expected him to be serious all the time. That was a relationship that would never work.

Then Marie laughed. "Of course! The height of responsibility. It's what I've always most admired about you. You would never do something foolhardy and risky for the sake of adventure."

Cordelia breathed a sigh of relief. Marie's irony suggested she knew him pretty well.

Rafe's eyes laughed back at Marie, and he reached out and

grabbed her around the waist. He tried to pull her closer, but she giggled and struggled out of his arms.

"You're supposed to be introducing me to your sister, remember?"

"I'm doing a rather poor job of it, aren't I?" He turned and gestured toward Cordelia. "May I present my sister, Princess Cordelia. Dellie, may I present my betrothed, Princess Marie."

The two girls smiled and gave each other small curtseys.

"It's an honor to be here, thank you for inviting me," said Cordelia, remembering her manners.

But a moment later, excitement swept her away, and she couldn't help adding, "I'm so happy to finally meet you. I've been wondering what you would be like the whole way here. I can't say I'm that excited to acquire yet another sister, but I know that if Rafe's chosen you, then you must be good fun."

A throat-clearing from behind them made her subside, yet another blush tinging her cheeks.

Rafe turned at the sound and cried, "Priscilla!" Ignoring the older woman's murmurs of protest, he embraced her enthusiastically.

She tut-tutted and shook her head, reaching up to straighten her hair.

"Really, Raphael, I was hoping you might have gained some decorum while you were away." Her tone suggested disapproval, but Cordelia could detect the glimmer of affection in her eye. It wasn't only among his younger sisters that Rafe was a favorite. Most of the palace staff loved him, too.

Priscilla was always reprimanding Rafe, and he was always laughing back at her. And, somehow, she seemed to love him for it. Cordelia sighed. She could only imagine the response if she tried to laugh at Priscilla. Instead she had to settle for occasionally getting Rafe to intervene on her behalf.

"It's lovely to meet you both," said Marie. She smiled at Priscilla and then turned back to Cordelia. "And unlike you, I only have a brother, so I've been looking forward to meeting Rafe's sisters. I can't imagine what life must have been like with seven of you! I asked Rafe if any of his Lanoverian friends were coming for the wedding, but he said none of you ever needed to make special friends. Not when you had each other."

Cordelia smiled. The young Lanoverian royals had earned something of a reputation for mischief in their childhood. Of course, Marie had grown up a royal, too. She must know how hard it was to form true friendships when you were so set apart. The Lanoverians had always relied on each other for company. Cordelia could no more imagine having only one brother than Marie could imagine being one of seven.

But then, from all reports, Marie's older brother, William, was as handsome and charming as princes were supposed to be. She had to admit to having indulged in a daydream or two about him during the travel to Northhelm.

She would be the only single princess at the wedding, and William would one day be a king. Now that Clarisse's husband, Prince Konrad of Rangmere, was dead, not even the oldest Lanoverian princess could claim that she would one day be a queen.

Imagine if William chose her. She would surpass all her sisters. Much more unlikely things had happened, after all. Prince Maximilian of Arcadia had even married a woodcutter's daughter.

The pretty daydream collapsed at the sound of another throat-clearing from behind her. Cordelia realized she still hadn't replied to Marie.

"That's kind of you. And as official representative of the Lanoverian royal family, I can assure you that we are delighted to welcome you into our ranks." There. That had sounded appropriately formal. Hopefully Priscilla would be pleased.

"Thank you, Cordelia—do you mind if I call you Cordelia?"

"No, not at all."

Marie slipped her arm through Cordelia's. "And please, call me Marie." She began to lead the way through the large entrance hall. "I'm going to show you to your room, and I've told Rafe he's not invited." She threw a teasing smile over her shoulder at Cordelia's brother. "I want to hear every embarrassing story you can remember from his childhood. He's already pried far too much information out of William and Ferdy, so I need ammunition of my own."

"Ferdy?"

"Ferdinand. He's the eldest son of the Marquis of Montrose and William's best friend. You'll meet them both soon enough, and then you'll see why I'm so glad to have another girl arrive. I've been rather outnumbered."

Her smile seemed warm and genuine, and Cordelia found it easy to smile back. She suspected Marie's comment was intended to put her at ease—it was impossible to imagine this tall, confident girl unable to hold her own. Cordelia appreciated it anyway. People didn't normally go out of their way to accommodate her.

Some of the warm glow from earlier returned. She just wished she could stop her mind returning to the man from the courtyard. Had the idea of speaking to her really been so off-putting that he had needed to run away?

Part of her wanted to ask Marie about him, but a bigger part wanted to forget the whole thing. She put him out of her mind yet again, but an uneasy feeling remained. Something else was bothering her. She traced the feeling back to its source—yet another memory from the courtyard. This time, it was the strange conversation she'd overheard from the carriage.

The whole thing had been so vague that she didn't see how she could ask Marie about it. Her curiosity and discomfort didn't abate, however.

The noble and his companion had been talking about arrivals and the other kingdoms. Perhaps if she turned the conversation in that direction, she could get some more information without actually mentioning the overheard exchange.

"I've been told to pass on all sorts of apologies from the rest of my family," she said to Marie. "They all wish they could be here, but it's too far for them to come."

"Of course, we all understand completely. They have to put their responsibilities first."

Cordelia chewed on the inside of her cheek. "Who else is coming?" she asked. "Are any of the other royals able to make it?"

"Yes, indeed! There will be quite a crowd of us." Marie looked pleased. "Max and Alyssa are coming from Arcadia. I can't wait to see them again. Have you met them?"

"No, my sister Celeste was the one who went to Arcadia. I heard the story, though, of course. A woodcutter's daughter! What's she like?"

"Absolutely lovely. And very sharp." Marie smiled reminiscently. "She's a bit of a bookworm, but I have firm plans to keep her out of the library for this trip. Who knows when we'll all have a chance to be together again?"

"I look forward to meeting her, then. Are any of the other Arcadians coming?"

Marie shook her head. "King Henry and Queen Eleanor have only recently completed an extended tour of their kingdom and didn't want to travel again so soon. Apparently the twins were wild to come, but their parents want to spend time with them, so they're stuck back in Arcadia, too." From her affectionate expression, Cordelia guessed that Marie liked the two younger princesses.

A sudden fear gripped her. "Is Clarisse coming?" She tried to keep the dread out of her voice. What would Marie think of her for hoping the answer was no?

Cordelia's older sister Clarisse was nice enough. As a small child, Cordelia remembered loving her and following her around. But the six-year age gap, combined with the serious nature of the older princess, had increasingly made her more like a second mother than a sister. It didn't help that Cordelia hadn't seen her in years—not since she had married the Rangmeran heir. Her husband had died the year before, but Clarisse had chosen to remain in Rangmere to support the new queen. Clarisse's presence in Northhelm would put a serious dampener on Cordelia's moment of independence.

Marie shook her head again, and Cordelia gave a little sigh of relief. "Queen Ava and King Hans are coming, and they asked her to stay in Rangmere as regent in their absence."

"So Ava and Hans will be here." Cordelia tried to picture the young rulers and failed. "Have you met them before? Are they very…" she wrinkled her nose "…Rangmeran?"

"I met Ava once, a long time ago. I didn't like her much back then, but I've heard she's changed a lot. And I've never met Hans."

Cordelia considered her words. They'd heard the same story in Lanover about Queen Ava's transformation. It was hard not to feel wary of the Rangmerans anyway, though. Rangmere had always seemed like such a strong, cold place, and the old king had been aggressive—a destabilizing force throughout the entire Four Kingdoms.

"Do you think it's true?" she asked. "Has she really changed?"

"I think she must have," said Marie slowly. "We had some recent trouble with rebels and Ava helped us. She didn't try to take advantage of our instability, and she hasn't asked for anything in return."

"Well, that's good, I guess." The news didn't entirely allay Cordelia's nerves at the thought of meeting the young queen. "And I suppose she did marry her personal guard. I can't imagine the old king doing something like that!"

"That's true. Although Hans is some sort of hero in Northhelm, I believe. I should ask Hanna about him before he arrives."

"Hanna?" Cordelia wished she was familiar with even one of the people Marie kept mentioning. She'd heard of the other royals, at least, but she'd never met any of them. And the North-helmians were entirely unfamiliar. It made her feel out of place and awkward.

"Hanna is Hans' sister. It turns out Hans' family actually live in Northhelm. I think that might be the real reason Ava and Hans are coming for the wedding, to be honest."

"Hanna and Hans?" Cordelia sighed. "I can see their parents had the same unfortunate tendency toward alliteration as ours."

Marie glanced sideways at her, as if checking her seriousness, and then almost sagged in relief. "Oh, thank goodness, you think it's ridiculous, too! You wouldn't believe how much trouble I have keeping you all straight. Rafe's explained it all more than once, and I still get confused. I've been so afraid I'd call you the wrong name when you arrived."

"Don't worry, it wouldn't be the first time." Cordelia rolled her eyes. "Rafe got seriously lucky. And my oldest brother, Frederic. But the rest of us..." She shook her head. "Clarisse, Cassian, Celeste, Cordelia, and Celine. What were my parents thinking?"

Marie laughed, and the two girls continued to chat amiably as they made their way through the palace. But the conversation only occupied half of Cordelia's mind. Arcadia was sending its heir, and Rangmere its rulers. Were they the arrivals the mysterious voices were waiting for? And, if so, what exactly did the voices mean when they called the royals 'infected'?

CHAPTER 3

*C*ordelia's room shone warmly thanks to a large fire in the stone fireplace. The flames lent a cozy effect to the stone walls, and the green velvet on the bed and the small sofa looked inviting. She ignored the maids who were unpacking her bags under Priscilla's watchful eye and crossed to the window.

The tall, arched opening gave her a good view of the snow that continued to fall. The sun had set and the whole city spread below her, lit by a golden glow from windows and the lanterns in the streets.

She gave a soft sigh.

"Is something wrong, Your Highness?" Priscilla once again demonstrated her ability to closely monitor Cordelia while appearing completely absorbed in some other task.

"Of course not. It's like a magical wonderland out there."

"Cold, wet stuff, snow." Priscilla sounded displeased. "I, for one, am glad we don't have it in Lanover."

Cordelia rolled her eyes. Trust Priscilla to focus on the practicalities when confronted with such a sight.

The older woman walked up behind her and looked over her

shoulder. "It is pretty, though." Her soft words surprised Cordelia. Perhaps her maid had some sensibility after all.

A knock on the door interrupted them before she could respond, and a footman announced the evening meal. Marie had offered to have a tray sent to her room if Cordelia felt too tired from the journey, but she had refused. She wanted to see Rafe again and hear all his news.

Or, at least, that was what she told herself. The fact that Prince William would be there had absolutely nothing to do with it. She glanced down at her elegant gown, glad that she'd taken the time to get changed. Unlike Northhelm, Lanover wasn't known for its formality, so Cordelia had endured several sessions from the etiquette master on northern customs before leaving. Her parents didn't want her disgracing her kingdom.

Given that Lanover was the richest of the Four Kingdoms, if there had been more time, Cordelia could have easily convinced her mother that she needed a whole new wardrobe for the trip. As it was, however, she had to be satisfied with her sisters' efforts. They had pooled their resources and come up with a respectable collection of gowns. The dress she wore now belonged to Celeste, and wearing it gave Cordelia confidence.

"You look very neat," said Priscilla approvingly.

Cordelia looked down at her ensemble again, assailed by doubt. Neat wasn't exactly the adjective she'd been going for. But after a moment she shook her head and stepped out of the room anyway. Hopefully Priscilla was simply being Priscilla.

Celeste had assured her that the gold would make her darker skin shine beside the pale northerners and bring out the golden flecks in her hazel eyes. She trusted her sister more than she trusted Priscilla.

Her confidence was rewarded when she entered the small, formal dining room used for family meals by the Northhelmian royals. The occupants of the room had grouped themselves around the fireplace at one end of the room, awaiting her arrival. When she appeared in the doorway, the tall young man standing with Rafe and Marie started visibly. All three of them moved toward her, but the stranger, who had to be Prince William, easily beat the other two. Cordelia hardly had time to register his presence before he was bowing over her hand.

"Princess." He dropped the lightest of kisses on her knuckles. "Word of your beauty has spread far and wide, but I see that the stories do not do you justice."

He looked up and met her eyes, his own a beautiful, sparkling blue.

She blushed. The moment was exactly how she had imagined, right down to his dark gold hair and broad shoulders. *Thank goodness none of the others came,* she thought and then felt guilty for her selfishness. Celine, in particular, had been so disappointed to be left behind.

"I expected you to come up with something better than that," said Marie, breaking the moment by sliding her arm into Cordelia's. "It's not very original."

"How can I be original when I'm overwhelmed by so much beauty?" asked William.

Cordelia blushed again. Thank goodness the golden tones of her skin at least partially masked the color. She didn't want the prince to think she was young and inexperienced, unused to compliments. Even if it was entirely true.

Well, unused to compliments from handsome princes at any rate. There were always people hanging around a palace, looking for a way to get close to the royal family, and willing to flatter a naïve younger prince or princess to do it. All of the Lanoverian royals knew how to recognize and ignore such cajolery. Getting attention from someone who had nothing to gain by it felt entirely different.

Marie led the way to her parents and introduced Cordelia to

King Richard and Queen Louise. The king gave her formal greetings, but the queen grasped her hand and smiled so warmly that she instantly put the princess at ease.

Marie then directed Cordelia to a place at the table, where she nearly dropped straight into her seat. Thankfully, Rafe caught her eye and gave her a warning look before she could embarrass herself. Remembering her lessons, she waited for the king to assist the queen and then sit himself before she pulled out her own chair.

The table was small enough that they were all able to carry on a single conversation, and Cordelia mainly kept quiet, focusing on her food and stealing occasional glances at Prince William. The prince, Rafe, and Marie kept up a steady stream of light-hearted jokes, and Cordelia found it easy to blend into the background. It was what she was used to doing at home, after all.

Only when the conversation turned to horses did she speak up.

"I wanted to bring Butterscotch, my riding mare, with me, but the journey was too long. I've been hoping you might have a horse I could ride here."

William's smile turned in her direction. "You enjoy riding? Then it would be my honor to provide you with a mount and ride with you. I could show you something of Northgate and its surrounds."

"I would like that." She opened her mouth to ask a question about the horse he had in mind for her, but the conversation had already moved on. She looked back down at her food and reminded herself of William's admiring expression at her arrival.

That moment had been everything she had dreamed it would be. So why did she still feel out-of-place?

The snow had stopped by the next morning, and only a light powdering remained to lend Northgate and the palace a storybook air. Cordelia dressed in her warmest outfit and found her way outside to admire the view. She ended up in a small garden behind the palace and sat down on an ornate bench next to a pond. The water hadn't completely frozen solid yet, but a thin film of ice spread across the surface. The sight made her shiver inside her warm jacket.

She plonked her bag on the bench beside her and turned her face up to the winter sun. She enjoyed the warmth of the rays, even while she mourned the inevitability of their melting the dusting of snow that still clung to the plants around her. In the absence of flowers, the white coating made the otherwise barren garden beautiful.

After several moments, she sighed and turned to her bag. Priscilla didn't approve of idleness, so Cordelia had brought her embroidery with her. Given her maid's propensity to appear at unwanted moments, it seemed wise to at least have one of her current work pieces out in view.

Rummaging through the contents, her hand hit something solid. She frowned. She had thought the bag felt heavier than usual. Pulling the stowaway out, she recognized Celeste's golden ball. She now remembered having put it in the embroidery bag to keep it safe.

It was an odd present, and she hoped Marie wouldn't find it too strange. Hopefully Rafe had already warned his betrothed about Celeste's curse. Cordelia examined it again, remembering her sister's words about magic and true love. Could it be true that the ball was a magic artifact? If it came from their godmother, it was possible.

She rolled it around in her hands. It certainly felt far too light for a ball made of gold. She threw it into the air, and it landed back in her hand with a satisfying thud. Smiling, she threw it again, higher this time.

When she reached to catch it a second time, her half numb fingers slipped, and the ball fell from her hand and straight into the pond. Light or not, it cracked the ice and disappeared from sight.

CHAPTER 4

*C*ordelia sat frozen, staring at the pond in dismay. After a moment, she dropped to her knees and dipped one hand into the water. Gasping, she pulled it back and tucked it under her arm. Her hand ached from the mere second it had spent in the icy water. She would never be able to plunge her whole arm in and feel around for the missing ball. She chewed the inside of her cheek.

"Have you lost something?" The deep, male voice sounded friendly. Cordelia stayed kneeling, reluctant to discover who it belonged to. Could she look more foolish?

She pushed up off the ground and back onto the bench before turning to greet the newcomer. To her relief, the man in uniform was hardly a handsome prince. In fact, he more closely resembled a frog. He stepped forward and his bow-legged gait only confirmed the impression made by his slightly bulbous eyes.

She blinked twice and then managed to compose herself. "I'm afraid I have. It was rather silly of me, but I've dropped a golden ball into this pond."

"Well, that's no trouble at all." The man stepped forward and waded into the water, breaking the rest of the ice. He felt around with his feet before exclaiming, "Ah-ha!" and reaching down into the water to retrieve the golden ball.

Smiling at her, he waded back out, dried the trinket on his jacket and presented it to her.

She stared up at him in astonishment before accepting it. He gave no indication of having felt the bone-chilling cold that had prevented her from retrieving the ball herself. She regretted her earlier uncharitable thoughts about his appearance. Someone from the Lanoverian royal family should know better than anyone that beauty is relative, and hardly a marker for inward virtue.

She looked down at the gold in her hands and wished she hadn't spent so much of her first few hours in Northgate feeling small and foolish. Perhaps the Lanoverians weren't actually to blame for always overlooking her.

"You'll have to find yourself some mittens." Her rescuer's words sounded friendly rather than condemning, and Cordelia found the courage to look up at him.

She had been so distracted by the strangeness of his features at first, that she had failed to notice the friendliness of his expression. Friendly and admiring, given the way his eyes lingered on her face.

"Mittens?"

"To keep your fingers warm."

"Oh, yes, of course..." she eyed the insignia on his jacket, "...Captain?"

"It's Major, I'm afraid." He sounded apologetic.

"Oh, sorry!" Cordelia hadn't had time to learn the different emblems of the Northhelmian military before leaving home, but she did know that a major outranked a captain. Thankfully her rescuer didn't seem like the easily offended type.

"That's quite all right." His cheerfulness was unabated. "I'm Ferdinand, by the way."

"Ferdinand? As in, Prince William's friend?"

Ferdinand looked a little alarmed. "That's me. I can't say my fame has ever preceded me before. I'm a little afraid to ask what he might have said about me."

"It was Princess Marie, actually. She just mentioned that you were a good friend of her brother's."

Ferdinand relaxed and smiled again. "Oh, that's all right, then. I won't have to punish William in that case."

Cordelia looked at him, startled. Was he allowed to joke about punishing the crown prince?

Ferdinand gave a chuckle at her expression. He waved at his insignia. "I'm not just his childhood friend, you know. I'm also his commanding officer. It's my solemn duty to whip him into shape and make sure he doesn't get too big for himself."

Cordelia relaxed and smiled back at him. "I'm sure you do an excellent job."

"I certainly do my best." The major gave a small bow. "And talking of my job, I really must get going. I'm overdue for patrol." He moved to the other side of the garden and untangled the reins of his horse from a bush. How had she missed the presence of the beautiful animal?

Ferdinand swung himself into the saddle, and his entire demeanor changed. All trace of the awkwardness that clung to his stride disappeared. He turned back toward her and reached up to doff his hat in her direction.

Cordelia stared at him, recognizing both his mount and the way he held himself on the horse. "Why, you're the man from yesterday!"

Ferdinand looked crestfallen. "I was hoping you wouldn't recognize me. I'm sorry for behaving so rudely. I didn't realize any of the royals had arrived yet, so you took me by surprise. I don't usually attend many palace functions, and I'm afraid I'm not very good at making small talk with beautiful princesses. When I saw you, I panicked. Not my finest hour." He shifted in the saddle. "When it comes to my squad, I have no problem knocking heads together. If only the same were true for lovely women, such as yourself."

Cordelia hid a laugh behind her hand. "You'd like to knock our heads together?"

"Oh! No! See, there you go—what did I say? I'm not one for pretty talk. William's the one you need for that sort of thing."

"Yes, the prince has been very kind." Cordelia hated the traitorous blush that crept up her face.

Sure enough, Ferdinand's eyes focused in on her cheeks. "Ah yes. I'm sure he's charmed you already." He sounded glum. "My parents wish I could be more like him. But just look at me. It's entirely out of the question." He waved vaguely in the direction of his face. "They only have themselves to blame, anyway," he muttered quietly.

Cordelia couldn't reassure him about his looks—he was the oddest-looking man she'd ever seen—but she knew all about feeling overlooked and outshone.

"At least they have expectations of you," she said, hoping to make him feel better. "My parents can't even remember my name correctly sometimes."

He grinned down at her, and the admiration in his eyes made her feel almost as good as Prince William's regard had done.

"I find that hard to believe," he said. "I know I could never mistake you for anyone else."

Cordelia sighed. "That's because you haven't met any of my sisters." She looked up and noticed an involuntary shiver shake his frame.

"Oh dear," she said, struck with worry. "You must be freezing! You can't go out on patrol wet through like that. Please tell me you'll go and change. I'd feel terrible if you got sick because of my clumsiness."

"It is rather chilly," Ferdinand admitted. "And I'd hate to cause you worry. I think I might dash back inside. If you'll excuse me, Your Highness."

"Cordelia, please."

Ferdinand smiled at her. "That's very kind of you to say, Your Highness."

Cordelia watched Ferdinand until he disappeared from sight and then returned the ball to her embroidery bag. She would stay inside until she had managed to acquire some mittens.

Making her way back through the gardens, Cordelia heard voices behind a large hedge. She paused to listen, trying to identify why they sounded so familiar.

"The Arcadians arrive in two days."

She stiffened. The mysterious speakers from the courtyard.

"They do indeed. But what I want to know is what you're doing lurking out here." The noble voice sounded less than pleased.

"I'm not doing any harm." The gruff notes in the second voice suggested displeasure. "I thought I'd keep an eye on the Lanoverian princess."

Cordelia put a hand over her mouth and tried to eliminate all sound of her breathing. He had been spying on her. She shuddered.

"I've told you already that we have no interest in her. You're not being paid to have your own ideas."

He paused, but the first voice had no reply to this. After a moment the noble continued. "For now, you need to ensure that the Arcadians are assigned to the expected set of rooms. And the Rangmerans, too, when they arrive in a couple of weeks. Don't get creative!"

"Yes, sir." The agreement sounded sullen, but apparently it satisfied the noble since the sound of receding footsteps followed the words.

Cordelia held her breath but neither of them came in her direction. When she was sure they had left the garden, she picked up her skirts and ran for the palace. Her earlier unease was confirmed. Something strange was going on in Northhelm.

CHAPTER 5

Still unfamiliar with the layout of the palace, it took Cordelia some effort to track Rafe down. It turned out that he was being fitted for his suit for the wedding, and Cordelia was only allowed into the room once she convinced the conscientious tailor's assistant that she was his sister.

When she entered, he held out both arms. "Well, sis, what do you think?"

The tailor frowned and pulled his arms back down before returning to pinning the bottom of the jacket.

"Very handsome," said Cordelia.

Rafe raised his eyebrows. "That's the best you can do? I'm disappointed."

Cordelia shook her head, not in the mood for her brother's joking ways. "I need to speak to you."

"What is it? Is something wrong?" Rafe's smile dropped away in response to her seriousness.

"Yes. No. I don't know. I think so?"

Rafe's grin crept back across his face. "You're not making much sense, Dellie."

Cordelia threw up her hands and sat down on a convenient chair. "I know. It's all a bit confusing."

"Well, this fellow should be finished soon. And then you can tell me all about it."

"Certainly, Your Highness," said the tailor. "I shall only be another moment."

He proceeded to take another twenty minutes, by the end of which Cordelia was bursting with impatience.

When the room was finally cleared, she poured out the story to her brother, repeating everything she had heard as exactly as possible. At the end of the story, she looked at her brother expectantly.

He frowned at her. "Well it was certainly wrong of the servant to be spying on you, but it sounds like he was reprimanded for it. Would you prefer to see him more severely punished?"

"What?" Cordelia eyed her brother, startled. "Punished? No, that's not what I mean at all. I'm worried. It sounds like they're planning something."

"Planning something?" Rafe smiled at her. "It sounds to me like they were planning the palace sleeping arrangements. Hardly a surprising occupation for palace servants expecting multiple royal delegations. With the wedding planned for Midwinter morning, the normal week's celebrations have been expanded. The whole thing sounds like it's getting rather excessive, to be honest." He smiled affectionately. "But Marie tells me to keep my nose out of it whenever I try to suggest such a thing."

Palace servants? Cordelia suddenly doubted herself. Had she misinterpreted the whole thing? Had her anxiety about being in a new place led her to put a dark interpretation on an innocent conversation?

Her instincts told her no. Rafe hadn't been there to hear the subtleties of their tone and inflection. And one of the voices had definitely belonged to a noble. As the sixth child of seven, Cordelia had always been a good listener. Unnoticed and unobserved, she had lurked through many a conversation not meant for her ears. She knew what she had heard.

But her hesitation seemed enough to convince Rafe. "Don't worry, Dellie. There's no need to fear every shadow. The royal guard have dealt with the rebel problem. Well, it was Marie who dealt with them mostly." He looked proud. "You don't have anything to worry about."

"But, Rafe…"

Cordelia's attempts to argue with him were cut off by a footman who appeared in the doorway. "Excuse me, Your Highnesses. But Princess Marie sent me to find you. She needs Princess Cordelia for a dress fitting."

Rafe jumped up. "We don't want to keep her waiting, then. She hates those things. I'll show you the way."

"Dress fitting?" Cordelia followed him down the corridor.

"Oh, sorry. I was meant to ask you about it. Marie wants you to be an attendant at the wedding. Along with Princess Alyssa and a few of the Northhelmian nobility."

"A bride's attendant? Really?" Cordelia's voice squeaked on the final word. She had been one years before at Clarisse's wedding, but she had been unexcited about it at the time. Everyone already had a difficult enough time noticing her apart from her sisters without them all being dressed identically, too. This time, however, would be different.

"Really." Rafe grinned in response to her expression. "I thought you'd be pleased." He opened a door and ushered her through. But when he tried to follow, his path was blocked by two determined looking seamstresses.

"Absolutely not, Your Highness," said one of them.

"Just for a moment," he said, flashing his most charming smile. "One kiss, and then I'll be gone."

"Absolutely not," repeated the second one.

Cordelia couldn't help smiling at their united front. "Sorry, Rafe, I don't like your chances this time."

She left him at the door still arguing with the two women and went looking for Marie.

"Cordelia! You've arrived, thank goodness." Marie rushed over and grabbed her arm, leaning down to whisper in her ear. "We've already had two fittings before this one and the wedding is still weeks away. I think if the royal seamstress had her way, we'd all do nothing but get in and out of dresses until Midwinter."

Two assistants hurried over and took charge of Cordelia before she could reply. And before she knew what was happening, she was out of her gown and being fitted for the dress she would wear at the wedding.

Marie had apparently chosen a pale, ice blue for her bride's attendants. A color that almost perfectly matched her own eyes and pale complexion.

"Sorry," she said, seeming to read Cordelia's mind. "It isn't the best fit with your coloring, is it? It's a good thing you're gorgeous enough that you'll look lovely in anything I put you in."

Cordelia opened her mouth to assure her that it didn't matter, but Marie had already disappeared, stolen away by yet another seamstress. Cordelia closed her mouth again and proceeded to sit, stand and move her arms as directed.

Eventually she was told to sit on a sofa. After that they appeared to forget about her, so she sat there for some time watching the bustle around her. It was hard to believe that a mere hour before, she'd been running through the palace in a panic. The emotion seemed distant now and out of place. Northhelm was a kingdom getting ready to celebrate, not a kingdom in crisis. Maybe Rafe was right, and she had let her imagination get the better of her.

"It's a bit much to take in, isn't it?" Another girl sat down beside her. "You look about as overwhelmed as I feel."

The young woman was beautiful, in the blue-eyed, golden-haired northern style, but more noticeable was the kindness in her eyes. She made Cordelia feel instantly at ease.

"It is a bit." Cordelia smiled at her. "I'm Princess Cordelia of Lanover, by the way. Are you one of the other attendants?"

"Yes, I am." The girl smiled hesitantly. "Although it feels a little surreal. I'm Lady Westruther, by the way." She shook her head, her expression bashful. "It still feels strange to say that."

"Oh, are you newly married?"

"Yes, the wedding was only a few months ago, and the whole thing was a complete whirl." She lowered her voice. "Six months ago I was one of the royal pastry chef's apprentices."

She laughed, an infectious, musical sound. "I don't know why I'm whispering—it's not exactly a secret."

"Sounds like a romantic story." Cordelia tried to keep any hint of jealousy out of her voice. Northhelm was her big chance for romance; she didn't need to be envious.

"Very romantic." Lady Westruther smiled dreamily. "But you should call me Hanna. Just about everyone does."

"Hanna?" Cordelia looked between her companion and Marie.

"Yes, I'm that Hanna," said the girl, following Cordelia's gaze. "I think I got asked to be an attendant as a Rangmeran counterpart to you and Princess Alyssa. Apparently Ava was out of the question because it isn't correct protocol to ask a reigning monarch to be an attendant.

"So now I'm a sort of stand-in princess. In case my life wasn't already strange enough! My parents don't know what to do with themselves now that their son has become a king. I can promise you, we never predicted any of this back when we were merely a guard and an apprentice."

"A fairy tale indeed," said Cordelia, more and more curious to hear their story.

"Anyway, I didn't mean to go on about myself! I came over because I saw the look in your eye, and I know what it feels like to feel a little lost and out-of-place. That's how I've been feeling for the last six months!"

"Well, from what Marie said, it sounds like we'll both get used to it pretty soon. Apparently we have endless fittings in our future."

Hanna sighed. "I'm rather afraid she's right. Although, I can understand why the seamstress wants to make sure everything is perfect. I would feel the same way if I was responsible for the cake."

From her expression, Cordelia guessed that Hanna would have preferred to be in charge of the cake than be an attendant. "Do you get to bake now that you're a lady?" she asked.

"Oh, yes. Stefan is wonderful about it. He loves my baking, and he always encourages me to take some time off in the kitchen whenever I start to feel overwhelmed. Mostly I only bake when we're in our own home, though. I don't get as much of a chance when we're staying at the palace." She pulled a face. "And with all the wedding preparations, I think we'll be based here until after Midwinter."

She shrugged. "Oh, well." Her look turned mischievous. "I can always sneak down to the palace kitchens to visit my old friends there. In fact, I'll see if I can make something delicious to bring to our next fitting."

"That sounds nice."

"I'll sneak it in past the seamstresses, and you'll have to promise not to spill anything on your dress!"

Cordelia giggled and promised, and the two girls parted in the friendliest of ways.

When she reflected on her day from her bed that evening, Cordelia concluded she'd had a productive time. After only one full day in Northgate, she'd already met both of the people Marie had mentioned in their first conversation.

But thoughts of Ferdinand brought with them thoughts of the second overheard conversation. Rafe had dismissed her concerns, but Cordelia couldn't do so as easily. A lot of important people were gathering for the wedding. What if danger lurked and only she realized it?

CHAPTER 6

*A*s she had predicted, the original snow had melted away. However, a second light snowfall from the night before had recoated the world in white. Cordelia admired the soft piles on the roofs and lanterns that she passed.

The powder softened the sound of the horses' hooves against the cobblestones until they got away from the palace and into a more frequented part of town. Here, the traffic had long since melted the snow on the road.

Cordelia rode a plodding old gelding, chosen no doubt with safety in mind. She would have to talk to Marie about finding a more interesting mount for their next ride. She didn't have the courage to tell William that she didn't appreciate his choice.

Thankfully the scene around her was so new and enchanting that she found it easy to forget the inadequacies of her horse. And she wasn't the only one enjoying the season, either. All around her, people smiled as they went about their business or called greetings to the young royals and their accompanying guards.

Children wove between the travelers, ducking away from any passing horses, their games and laughter floating above the ordinary sounds of the day. They all wore mittens and cute little knitted caps, and Cordelia smiled as she gazed down at her own gloved hands. Marie had loaned her a soft pair of leather riding gloves, and her fingers were much more comfortable than they had been on her last excursion.

They reached a large cobbled square, surrounded on all sides by tall, elegant buildings of gray stone. A bustling market had been set up in the square and most of the stalls sold seasonal delicacies or gift items. In Northhelm, as in all the Four Kingdoms, it was traditional to give gifts to loved ones on Midwinter morning.

William signaled for Cordelia to dismount, and Marie and Rafe followed suit. They handed their reins to one of the guards and wended their way into the market.

Cordelia sniffed the air. "Something smells delicious."

William grinned at her, and her heart melted a little. He had just returned from patrol, and he looked particularly handsome in his military uniform.

"Wait here," he said and disappeared.

"What's he doing?" she asked Marie.

"You'll see." From Marie's anticipatory smile, Cordelia guessed she both knew and approved of her brother's intentions.

She wandered a few steps away to examine a stall of intricate wooden carvings. Although she would be away for Midwinter, she had resolved to bring back presents for all her family.

Marie followed to peer at the wares over her shoulder.

"This is pretty." She picked up a small wooden deer and turned it over in her hands. She looked up at Cordelia. "Your own people probably warned you but, just in case...Northhelm holds firmly to its traditions. And according to our customs, the giving and receiving of a gift between a man and a woman signifies an engagement. Even at Midwinter." She smiled. "It's a popular time for betrothals."

Cordelia suspected from her tone of voice that a story lay

behind the warning. Before she could ask about it, however, a call of greeting interrupted them. Two familiar figures approached, both loaded down with delightful smelling burdens. The contrast between the prince and his best friend was almost comical, but Cordelia still felt pleased to see Ferdinand.

"Look who I found!" said William. "And a good thing, too, or I would have run out of hands." Looking proud of himself, he handed Cordelia a mug and a paper cone before distributing the same items to the rest of the group.

Ferdinand stepped up beside her. "It's mulled wine," he said quietly. "And roasted chestnuts. Here, let me hold the chestnuts for you."

She smiled at him gratefully and wrapped both hands around her mug. The warmth managed to seep through both the cup and her gloves, and her fingers tingled pleasantly. She inhaled the scent and took a sip.

Ferdinand held the cone out toward her, and she carefully selected the plumpest looking chestnut. The delicious flavors complemented the warm beverage. "Where are yours?"

"I only bumped into William after he'd completed his purchase. And a good thing, too, or we wouldn't have had enough hands even between the two of us." He smiled at her. "And I'm glad to miss out if it means I can be of service."

"Thank you," said Cordelia, touched by his thoughtfulness. "You can share mine, if you like."

"Well, I won't say no to that," said Ferdinand, popping a chestnut in his mouth. "They've always been a favorite of mine, to be honest."

"So now I know why you were so happy to help me out!"

"You have to be resourceful when you're in the military. It's considered an excellent trait." He helped himself to another chestnut.

"Hey!" William had turned from his conversation with Marie

and Rafe in time to see his friend's action. "I bought those for the princess."

"Ah, but as your superior officer, I maintain the right to requisition your supplies at any time." He crunched down on another nut. "And to rectify any ungallant behavior that I observe."

"Ungallant? Ungallant!"

"How was Princess Cordelia supposed to eat her chestnuts when she had both hands full? Plus, she needed her hands free to wrap around her mug—everyone knows mulled wine is for warming your hands as well as your stomach." He patted his enraged-looking friend on the back. "Don't worry, old chum, that's why I'm a major and you're still a private."

"I'm the prince!"

Ferdinand shrugged. "Well, there wasn't anything they could do about that now, was there?"

Cordelia, who'd been covering her smile with her hand, let out a little giggle.

"It's a good thing he has you around to keep him in line, Ferdy," said Marie.

Ferdinand gave a small half bow. "I do my best, Your Highness."

"Why you, you…" William slung his arm around his friend's neck and pulled it tight, giving him a small shake.

Ferdinand laughed and pushed his friend off. "Don't worry, my superiors have assured me they have high hopes for you. With a bit more effort, you might make it to lieutenant one day."

Marie gave a loud snort of laughter.

William drew himself up to his full height and turned his back on them both. "Please ignore my friend and my sister, Princess. I would be honored to hold your chestnuts for you."

"I'll bet you would," said Ferdinand, carefully choosing another nut. He made no move to hand the cone over.

William eyed him off but apparently decided that scuffling over the treat would be beneath his dignity. Instead he offered

Cordelia his arm and began to point out stalls of interest. Ferdinand fell into step on her other side while Rafe and Marie drifted some way behind, their arms entwined and their heads close together.

Cordelia chose a beautiful pair of gloves to replace the ones she had borrowed and then stopped at a stall selling perfume in small crystal bottles. She occupied herself with smelling the samples on display while the stall holder dealt with a voluble merchant's wife who had arrived before them. The princess had nearly decided on a particularly nice scent for her mother, when the other customer finally made her selection.

The stall holder, full of smiles, turned to wrap the purchased bottle in soft silk. As he did so, a rough looking man approached the back of the stall and said something quietly to the parfumier. The stall holder had his back to the merchant's wife, but Cordelia, standing to the side, could still see his face. His smile fell away instantly, and a dark look came into his eyes when he saw the man. He answered him shortly, and even more quietly, and his response brought a dangerous look into the newcomer's face.

Cordelia wondered idly who he could be. Perhaps the stall holder had hired him to perform some manual labor for him, and the other man felt he had been cheated? It made sense that the parfumier would be angry to be confronted at the market in front of potential buyers.

The stall holder finished wrapping the woman's purchase and turned back around, his face transformed back into a smile. After thanking the woman and sending her on her way, he turned to Cordelia. He extended a standard greeting, his gaze assessing the value of her wardrobe and his expression turning greedy. He spared a small glance at her escort and then did a double take.

"Your Highness! What an honor. How may I serve you?" His attention had fixed firmly on William, but Cordelia noticed that his smile no longer reached his eyes. If anything, they looked nervous.

Her eyes flashed to the rough-looking worker at the back of the stall and then followed his gaze to the parfumier's back. She couldn't see what he was looking at. Carefully, so as not to draw attention to herself, she eased to the side. Picking up a new bottle to mask her intentions, she looked behind the stall holder. His arms were tucked behind his back, but his hands were waving frantically, gesturing for the other man to be gone.

"I have the finest perfumes in Northgate, Your Highness. Are you looking for a gift, perhaps?"

Was it her imagination, or had the parfumier put the slightest emphasis on 'Your Highness'? The worker, who had been glaring sullenly at the stall holder's hand signals, gave a small jerk at the words, before swinging around and lumbering away.

Well, that was odd, thought Cordelia, watching his departure. She looked down at the perfume in her hands, her brow creased. Somehow she wasn't in the mood for shopping anymore. She shook her head in response to William's questioning eyebrows. She would buy something for her mother another day.

William, transformed by the presence of the parfumier into a serious and dutiful prince, extricated them all from the stall with grace.

"That was well done," commented Ferdinand as they made their way back toward their waiting guards and horses. "I didn't think we were going to get out of there without either buying something or offending the man."

"Did either of you notice anything odd about him?" asked Cordelia.

"Odd?" William laughed. "He was rather excessive in his enthusiasm for his wares—and in his enthusiasm for my rank. But, unfortunately, that's not all that uncommon for a merchant in the market. Don't they behave like that in Lanover?"

"No, it wasn't that. It was the other man. The rough-looking one."

William shrugged. "I'm sorry, I didn't notice another man. But if you decide you want one of the perfumes after all, I can send one of the footman from the palace down for it. You don't need to deal with him again."

"Oh, no, it's not that," said Cordelia, but they had arrived at their horses, and William didn't seem to hear her.

Marie and Rafe had reappeared, and they all began to mount. In the confusion, Cordelia let the matter drop, still not sure what she had seen.

Ferdinand appeared at her side to give her a leg-up. "Are you all right, Princess Cordelia?"

"Yes, I'm fine." She frowned. "But I think something strange was going on at that stall. I know the parfumier seemed obsequious when he recognized Prince William but, at the same time, I thought he seemed uncomfortable with us being there."

Ferdinand frowned at her. "You think he had something to hide?"

"I don't know. Maybe?"

"I'll ask around, if you like," he offered. "See if anyone knows anything about him."

"It might be nothing," said Cordelia, afraid she was making a big deal out of nothing.

"Don't worry, Your Highness, I'll keep it quiet."

The group of riders began to move, and Cordelia glanced over her shoulder at the receding figure of Ferdinand. He was watching them ride away with a look of thoughtful concern. A pressure she hadn't even noticed lifted. Someone was taking her seriously.

CHAPTER 7

*W*hen they rode back through the palace gates, chaos confronted them. Riders and grooms crowded around several carriages, and servants carrying bags weaved through the milling horses.

"Woah!" Rafe, who was leading the way, pulled his horse to a sudden halt. "It looks like someone else has arrived." He stood up in his stirrups, trying to get a better view. "I think that's an Arcadian carriage."

"Alyssa!" Marie slid down and ran off into the crowd.

Rafe swung down as well and captured her reins. He started waving for a groom, clearly eager to be off after Marie. Cordelia made no move to follow their lead. She felt much safer on the back of her horse than fighting her way through the crowd.

Rafe finally caught someone's attention and managed to offload both horses. As he disappeared, William pulled his mount up next to Cordelia.

"I take it that's Princess Alyssa." At Cordelia's questioning expression, he pointed toward the other side of the courtyard.

She followed his arm and managed to locate Marie who was embracing a shorter girl with a bright smile. A tall young man

44

with dark hair and brilliant blue eyes watched them fondly. She could only assume he was Prince Maximilian.

Rafe appeared at their side just as a piercing scream yanked her attention to the far side of the courtyard. A loud whinny rang through the suddenly hushed crowd, and then pandemonium broke out.

A large chestnut stallion reared. A groom went flying, colliding with a maid carrying a large case. Both disappeared from view.

Several people rushed to help them before screaming and scattering as the chestnut charged forward. Cordelia followed the animal's trajectory and gasped. The horse was racing straight for the four royals who had turned toward the commotion.

William swore and spurred his own horse forward, but he had no chance of making it through the crowd in time.

"William, stop!" she screamed, worried he would trample someone.

He groaned and pulled up, recognizing the danger.

Cordelia's eyes flew back to the charging horse. She gasped again.

Prince Max had jumped directly in the path of the charging stallion, wildly waving his arms. In only a second the horse would be on top of him, and he would be trampled beneath its hooves. But then he roared, the sound loud even above the hubbub of the panicking crowd.

The animal hesitated and swerved aside at the last possible second, its mad dash slowing.

Rafe darted forward, taking the opportunity to grab the end of a rope trailing from its halter. He hauled back on it, throwing his whole body into the effort. The horse's head pulled to the side, and it reluctantly came to a halt, its sides quivering.

Cordelia slumped in her saddle and drew a long, unsteady breath.

A shaking groom stepped forward and took charge of the

animal. Cordelia wasn't sure who looked more scared—the groom or the horse. Was he afraid of the chestnut or afraid of losing his position? Perhaps he had been responsible for the stallion.

In another moment they had both disappeared from sight, and two smaller hives of activity began to form within the courtyard. One centered around the royals as both Arcadian and Northhelmian officials rushed forward to check their safety. The second crowd surrounded the injured servants.

Several doctors and nurses appeared from the palace and directed some of the servants to prepare stretchers. The groom sat up, and the maid gripped the hand of one of the nurses, so they were alive at least.

The sound of ringing hooves behind her made her flinch. And she wasn't alone. Several heads in the courtyard whipped around to identify the source of the noise. Turning, she saw Ferdinand racing toward the palace on a mount she hadn't seen before.

He pulled up beside her and scanned the crowd. His eyes picked out Marie, Rafe, and then William, who had abandoned his horse and nearly made it to his sister's side.

"I was already on my way back when I heard there was some sort of accident. I borrowed this horse and rushed here as fast as I could. What happened?" he asked Cordelia, his eyes now on the injured. The voice of one of the doctors rang across the courtyard, directing the servants as they gently lifted the patients onto the stretchers.

"It was a horse. A huge stallion. I don't know if it was Northhelmian or Arcadian, but it got loose in the courtyard."

"And charged the crowd?" Ferdinand sounded incredulous.

"It looked more spooked than aggressive. But I didn't hear any unusual noises that might have set him off. It seems odd indeed that such a nervous animal would be brought into a busy courtyard like this."

"More than odd." Ferdinand narrowed his eyes as he stared

across at the large royal stable. "Criminal, more like it. If you'll excuse me, I need to have a word with the head groom."

He nodded at her politely, but his eyes didn't leave the stable building.

Cordelia fought disappointment as he rode through the crowd at a careful walk. She could hardly blame him for his distraction, given the situation. She was being nothing but foolish to even notice his lack of attention, let alone to miss the admiration in his gaze.

"Are you all right, Princess?" William appeared at her side, as if summoned by her thoughts, his handsome face focused on her.

"Yes, yes, I'm fine. But what about those servants?"

"The groom has a rather nasty cut but is otherwise unhurt. Unfortunately, that's because the maid broke his fall." He grimaced. "She broke her leg. All in all, it could have been worse." He frowned, and his eyes strayed toward the stables. "I can't imagine who brought a beast like that into the courtyard at such a time."

"Ferdinand said the same thing. He's already gone to speak to the head groom."

"Oh, has he?" William's expression lightened. "I didn't see him arrive. I should have guessed it, though. He always manages to be right where he's most needed."

He smiled his charming smile again and offered his hand to help her down. "Come inside, and I'll introduce you to Max and Alyssa."

As they made their way into the palace, the rest of the courtyard slowly emptied as well. The injured servants were long gone, and the last of the carriages rolled toward the stables. Cordelia followed with her eyes, but Ferdinand failed to reappear. What excuse was the head groom giving him?

The other royals had gathered inside the entrance hall. Marie and Alyssa's conversation flew so fast Cordelia could barely keep up, so she turned to Max and Rafe.

"That was very brave of you. Both of you."

"I didn't do much," said Rafe with his usual good nature. "The credit belongs to Prince Max here."

"Still, I'm glad you're all right." Cordelia couldn't resist giving her brother a squeeze. She appreciated his solidity after the fright. He hugged her back and then pushed her away.

"Dellie, this is Prince Maximilian from Arcadia. Max, this is my sister, Princess Cordelia."

"It's lovely to meet you," said Max.

"And you." Cordelia gave a small curtsey. She felt almost shy beneath the intensity of his blue eyes. "I've heard a lot about you." Her eyes flicked to Alyssa.

"Ah yes," he smiled broadly, following her gaze. "I think the whole of the Four Kingdoms has heard about our tale. What could be more romantic than a prince marrying a woodcutter's daughter?"

Cordelia studied his face a little wistfully. She wished someone would look at her with the sort of love she saw blazing in his eyes when they rested on his wife. "So it's true, then? She really is a woodcutter's daughter?"

"Absolutely." Max frowned. "That doesn't really sum her up, though. Her mother was a merchant's daughter and taught Alyssa to love books almost as much as she does people. She's well-read, intelligent, beloved by most of our kingdom, and godmother-chosen as well." He looked back down at me and chuckled. "But yes, her father did chop wood for a living."

"I'm sorry," said Cordelia, "I didn't mean any disparagement of Princess Alyssa."

"No, no, of course not." Max shook his head. "I'm the one who should apologize. I just want the rest of the kingdoms to appreciate her as much as Arcadia does." He raised his voice. "Alyssa! Come over here and meet Rafe's sister."

Marie looked up from their tête-à-tête. "He's right, I shouldn't be monopolizing you." She led the way toward the others and introduced the two princesses. And then frowned.

"William, we should send someone to check on those injured servants. And to the stables to find out what in the kingdoms happened with that horse."

"Already done," said William. "I talked to the doctors myself, and Ferdy has gone to see the head groom."

"Oh, good. That's taken care of, then." She turned back to the Arcadians. "Let me show you to your rooms. I'm sure you'd like to freshen up before the evening meal."

Cordelia trailed along behind the rest of the royals, her mind on Ferdinand. William and Marie trusted him like a brother, and that gave her confidence that she had made the right decision to leave the matter of the parfumier in his hands as well.

She wished she could shrug off the incident in the courtyard as quickly as the rest of them seemed to have done. The sound of the poor horse's terrified whinny, and the equally terrified screams of the servants, kept ringing in her head. The haunting sounds did nothing but strengthen her sense of impending danger.

CHAPTER 8

"*E*xcuse me, Your Highness. Before you leave, I need to know which dress you would like to wear to the ball tonight."

"Ball?" Cordelia, who had nearly escaped the room, popped back through the doorway. "Did you say ball, Priscilla?"

"I did, Your Highness."

"How did I not know about the ball tonight?" She plonked onto her bed and began running through her gowns in her mind.

"I couldn't say, Your Highness." Priscilla paused and then seemed to unbend a little. "I believe it is in honor of the Arcadian heir."

"My first Northhelmian ball. I wonder who I'll dance with." William seemed like a given. What would it feel like to be held in his arms?

Unbidden, an image of Ferdinand filled her mind. She pictured him in a ballroom and couldn't prevent a small giggle escaping.

"Is there something amusing about the idea of a ball, Your Highness?" Priscilla raised her eyebrows.

Cordelia schooled her expression back into seriousness. "I'm just excited to have the chance to dance again." Next to riding, dancing was Cordelia's favorite activity.

To her surprise, Priscilla's face actually softened into a small smile. "May I suggest the red dress? The one Celine had made right before we departed."

Cordelia considered the suggestion. She had been surprised when her younger sister had offered the dress. It was a striking color and a bold dress—the sort of thing her precocious younger sister loved, and the fourteen-year-old hadn't even had a chance to wear it yet.

Cordelia suspected that their mother might have had something to do with the generous donation.

"I believe Her Majesty was glad to see the dress sent with you," said Priscilla, apparently reading Cordelia's mind. "I think it would be perfect for your Northhelmian debut."

Cordelia examined her maid closely. Was Priscilla making a joke at Celine's expense? A subtle one, certainly, but… She shook her head in amazement. Unexpected.

"Sounds perfect." She immediately scrapped her plans for the day. First she was going to find Rafe and demand to know why he hadn't told her about the ball. Then, she needed to get ready. She almost skipped out of the doorway. In a few short hours she would be dancing again.

A murmur ran through the crowd as Cordelia descended the stairs into the ballroom. The herald had announced her, and a fanfare had even sounded, as she stepped through the doors to the top of the sweeping staircase.

By the time she reached the bottom step and placed her hand into William's, she had already determined to thank Priscilla. She was turning out to be a better personal maid than Cordelia had expected. The woman's dress choice had been masterful.

The prince swept her into a dance, and her spirits soared along with her feet. She only listened to William's compliments with half attention, too busy marveling at the ballroom. The dance floor took up less space than the Lanoverian main ballroom, but it was much taller. She tipped her head back and marveled at the ceiling, a full two stories above her head. The large crystal chandeliers glowed in the distance.

"You're not listening to me, are you?" She could hear the laugh in William's voice.

"Sorry. I'm distracted by the beautiful room."

He looked around as if noticing it for the first time. "This is nothing. Wait until you see it decorated for the Midwinter Masquerade."

"What's that?" She was pretty sure just from the name that she was going to love it.

"It's a big masked ball that Mother and Father always throw on Midwinter's Eve. I thought maybe we wouldn't have it this year, since the wedding is the next day, but with so many visitors it's going to be a bigger event than ever."

"It sounds delightful."

"A whole team work on decorating the ballroom. There will be evergreen boughs everywhere and holly. And maybe even some mistletoe." His eyes twinkled at her mischievously.

Cordelia repressed a blush.

"But that's still weeks away. I noticed you haven't been out riding since the unfortunate incident when the Arcadians arrived. I hope it hasn't put you off."

"Oh, no. I love to ride. I've been otherwise occupied."

"Well, you must go riding with me again, then."

Cordelia gathered her courage. "I would enjoy that, thank you. Perhaps…perhaps a different mount, though?"

William grimaced. "I shouldn't have gone for safe, should I? In my defense, I thought it was better safe than sorry."

"I understand. Perhaps if I tell you a little bit about my horse at home?"

"To tell you the truth, I'm not really the one to talk to."

Cordelia carefully kept her smile in place. She would have enjoyed talking about Butterscotch.

"I don't have much talent for choosing riding mounts for others," William continued. "I'll leave the job to Ferdy next time. Which is what I should have done from the beginning. He's the horse enthusiast between us." He smiled down at her. "I'm very sorry to prove such a disappointment, Princess."

Cordelia smiled back. After all, no girl could find a smile like that disappointing. Could they?

Two hours later she eased herself into a seat on the edge of the ballroom. She had been dancing non-stop, and her feet needed a break. She wriggled them out of her dancing slippers and stretched them out, hiding both the movement and her empty shoes beneath her large skirts.

She hadn't danced with William again since that first dance, but neither had she wanted for competent and admiring dance partners. In fact, she had been claimed by an eager young gentleman before the music from her first dance had completely died away. William had handed her over readily enough, and she had watched his face out of the corner of her eye for any discontent. But he had remained as cheerful as he had been throughout their dance.

She had tried to consider her own feelings on the matter, but her new partner was such a skilled dancer that she had been swept up in the movement before she had time to reach a conclusion. Heart searching would have to wait for later.

Now she had a quiet moment but was much too exhausted for deep thoughts. Instead she occupied herself with watching the swirling silks and satins and debating whether it would be worth the energy to get up and go in search of a drink.

She looked around, but not a footman was in sight. She gave a soft sigh and started sliding her feet back into her slippers.

"Good evening, Your Highness."

Startled, her foot slipped, and her shoe tipped over onto its side. She chewed the inside of her cheek and tried to right it again without letting her movement show.

Her mind half occupied by the activity, she looked around for the speaker, trying to muster a civil greeting.

"Oh, Ferdy, it's just you." Her words slipped out without thought, as her foot slid into the slipper. She gave him a big smile to cover up her inadvertent informality.

Thankfully his return smile seemed genuinely pleased. "Yes, just me, I'm afraid. I've been watching you dance. I mean…" his eyes got even rounder than usual, and he looked uncomfortable, "…I've been watching all the dancers." He looked down at his feet. "I'd ask you to dance myself, but I'm afraid I'm rather hopeless at it."

Cordelia could well imagine. She tried to show her lack of judgment in her smile. "To be honest, it wasn't a dance but a drink that I was wishing for."

Ferdinand straightened. "Well, that I can easily provide. I'll be back in a moment."

He disappeared among the dancers, and Cordelia sat back and closed her eyes, hoping to keep any more dance partners away.

Surely no more than a minute had passed before a clearing throat made her eyes fly open again.

"You're back already, that was quick!"

Ferdinand bowed. "I'm glad to be of service." He paused as if considering his next words. "You look a little warm, Princess Cordelia. Would you like to walk for a moment on the balcony?"

He gestured toward the side of the ballroom opposite the main stairs. The wall was lined with tall glass doors which provided access to a large marble balcony. Several of the doors stood open to allow some of the cold night air into the room.

"Thank you, that would be lovely." Cordelia rose to her feet, grateful she had managed to get her feet back into her slippers, and took Ferdinand's arm. Awkwardly they made their way past the dancers and into the night.

"Ahh," she said, tipping her head back and closing her eyes again. "This is nice." The freezing air felt pleasant against her flushed face.

She moved over to the railing and peered over the edge. It was more of a terrace than a true balcony, a few shallow steps leading down into the garden. Glancing around she saw with relief that they weren't the only dancers seeking relief in the winter night. Agreeing to come out hadn't been an error in protocol, then.

Slowly they wandered toward the farthest end.

"Do you usually attend all the royal balls just so you can stand in a corner and watch?" She glanced at him through her lashes, wondering if he would find the question too cheeky.

"See, there you go." He sighed. "I knew I was going to look like a fool. Normally I schedule my patrol shifts so they coincide with functions like these. Gives me a handy excuse." He shook his head. "Doesn't work at Midwinter, though. There are far too many balls and parties and dances. Which is why I always go home to visit my parents on their estates for Midwinter."

"Except for this year?"

He shrugged. "Marie is more than my childhood friend, she's also my princess. Which makes staying in the capital for her wedding compulsory. Unfortunately, there are some things that can't be avoided when you're the son of a Marquis." His eyes narrowed. "William is getting a rather unholy amusement out of the whole thing."

"Well, I'm sure you're not as bad a dancer as you think," said Cordelia, trying to be encouraging.

"Worse, I'm afraid," said Ferdinand.

The unexpected stab of disappointment took Cordelia by surprise. She normally never chose to walk outside or sit out more than a dance or two at most. But she was enjoying her time with Ferdinand. She felt comfortable, no longer on show. She would have liked to dance with him.

They had reached the far end, and the light was so dim, she could barely make out his features. For an unthinking moment, she wanted to lean into him and feel his arms around her. The winter air had become less and less pleasant, and she would appreciate his warmth. She swayed in his direction before pulling herself up straight.

Looking up, she found his eyes fixed on her face. Could he see her properly in the gloom? Had he been able to read her expression?

He cleared his throat. "Your glass is empty, Princess Cordelia. Allow me to refill it for you."

He whisked the glass from her hand and was gone before she could formulate a coherent answer. She backed up against the wall and sunk onto a low bench. What had come over her? Thank goodness Priscilla hadn't been present to witness her foolishness.

"You again!"

Cordelia's head jerked up. The words had come from the garden below the balcony. And she recognized the voice. It was the third time she had heard it.

"Yes, me." The second voice was familiar, too. The same pair, then. Were the unknown noble and his underling following her around? Or was it just luck that put her in a place to overhear all their conversations?

"This is the fifth time you've accosted me in the last two days. It has to stop, now." Maybe not all of them, then. She strained her ears to hear whatever came next, while wishing she could have heard the last four conversations.

"I'm trying to make sure there aren't any mistakes." The second voice sounded sullen.

"Mistakes?" The noble's voice was slippery and dangerous. "If you want to talk about mistakes, let's talk about the debacle in the courtyard the other day."

Cordelia tried to hold her breath in the long silence that followed, afraid they might hear it.

The noble's sinister chuckle broke the stillness. "Nothing to say? I thought as much. All you need to do is your job, and we won't have any more trouble. Do you understand?"

The clear sound of someone spitting onto the ground floated over the bushes. "I understand."

Surely his reluctance sounded as loudly to the noble as it did to her.

"Oh, and don't go accosting anyone else, either. The parfumier told me you turned up at his stall while the prince was there."

Cordelia stiffened. So the second man was the rough looking worker from the perfume stall. Finally she had a face to put to one of the voices.

"I didn't realize it was the prince, or I would have stayed away, wouldn't I?"

"Would you?" The noble sounded bored now. "Perhaps you're crediting yourself with too much good sense." He sighed. "I'm beginning to think we made the wrong choice when we hired you."

The other man swallowed audibly. "Don't you worry now, there won't be any more mistakes."

"There had better not be."

A single pair of footsteps climbed the stairs onto the balcony, approaching the spot where Cordelia waited. She shrank into the shadows.

CHAPTER 9

A tall man swept past her into the ballroom. Thankfully he didn't bother looking around the dim balcony, or he might have seen her cowering against the wall of the palace. She caught his profile as he passed one of the bright doorways and filed the image away. She would recognize him again if she saw him.

She waited, breathless, but the second man must have exited through the garden. She let out a sigh of relief. That had been close.

She leaped up. She had to find Rafe. Surely he would believe her now.

The light and warmth of the ballroom had barely enveloped her when she collided with William.

He steadied her. "There you are! I think we're due for another dance."

She didn't even notice his charming smile this time, too busy looking for Rafe.

"You seem perturbed, Princess. Why don't you tell me what's troubling you while we dance?"

She stopped and focused on him. Perhaps he was right. It was his kingdom after all. He should be informed if danger lurked in it. Nodding, she let him sweep her onto the dance floor.

"Well?" he prompted after a few steps of silence.

"It's a bit of a long story." Uncertainty gripped her. How could she explain it so it made sense?

"I don't think we'll scandalize anyone too greatly if we dance the next two dances." He smiled encouragingly at her.

She took a deep breath and poured out the whole story, from the overheard conversation in her carriage when she first arrived in Northgate, to the one outside the ballroom.

When she finished, William looked more uncomfortable than worried, and her heart sank. What had Rafe told the North-helmians about his little sister? Had he told them she was observant and had excellent hearing and recall? Or that she was young and flighty and liked dresses and balls?

"The accident with the stallion was certainly unfortunate," he said slowly. "But the injured servants will recover well enough. I'm sorry that you've been feeling uncomfortable here, but you did say the noble was rebuking the servant for the courtyard incident, didn't you? That doesn't sound too ominous." He looked thoughtful. "Perhaps you've stumbled upon the guilty groom. I can't say it would surprise me that neither he nor his noble master have been willing to own up to it."

"So you haven't found who's responsible?"

"No, but then the whole courtyard was in chaos, and, as I said, it's not exactly surprising that the guilty party doesn't want to own up. Thank you for letting me know. Can you point the noble out?"

"I've been keeping an eye out for him, but I think he must have left the ballroom."

"Well, if you see him again, can you let me or Marie know? We'll know who he is. And then I can talk to him about covering the medical expenses for the injured servants. It's the least he can do, really."

Cordelia stared at him. He wanted to tip the man off that she had overheard his conversations, and they knew who he was? She wouldn't be pointing the man out to him if that was his intention.

"I'll keep my eyes open." She kept her words deliberately vague.

"Thank you, and don't worry too much if you don't see him again. The crown will help the servants with the expenses if he isn't found. There's no long-term harm done."

Cordelia barely refrained from narrowing her eyes at him. Why did she get the feeling that he didn't believe she would be able to point the man out?

Annoyed, she looked away, her gaze glancing over the crowd. A lone figure caught her attention.

Ferdinand stood to the side of the room, his eyes fixed on Cordelia and William. One of his hands gripped her now full glass, but the other was clenched into a fist. She felt a wave of guilt. He had gone to fetch her another drink, and she had abandoned him. She hoped he hadn't been worried or spent long looking for her.

His face didn't look angry. Instead, a mix of sadness and longing transformed his strange features, and the sight filled her with an emotion too complex to name.

The song finished and William spun her around one last time. When she stopped, her eyes landed on Priscilla. The maid had appeared from nowhere and was wearing a familiar expression. The face of a chaperone who was determined to do her duty, regardless of the difficulty of her charge.

Cordelia curtsied to William and escaped to Priscilla's side with unexpected gratitude. As the young and old woman left the ballroom together, she wasn't sure which of them was more surprised by her compliance.

❧

Cordelia spent half the night tossing and turning. After a while, she decided she was angry with William for not taking her more seriously. And, if she was honest, she was disappointed that the handsome prince wasn't providing the perfect romance she had envisioned.

But if she had thought this acknowledgment would give her enough closure to fall asleep, she was soon disabused of the notion. Having the faces to go with the voices made the unknown men harder to ignore. She kept replaying the scene with the stallion, trying to remember if the rough-looking servant had been present. But it was a few days ago now, and she hadn't been looking for him at the time. She just couldn't be sure.

Eventually she decided that she would try talking to Rafe again. And after that she spent at least an hour going over the whole story in her mind and trying to put together a compelling case. She was going through it for the fourth time when she finally started to drift into sleep.

But as her thoughts gave way to dreams, it was Ferdinand's face that filled her mind. Him returning to the balcony and finding her gone, looking for her and finding her dancing with William, made her a little sick.

She wasn't that person. The one who abandoned a friend without a thought because a handsome prince walked past. She had to find him and explain what had happened.

Unfortunately, William had already talked to Rafe before she found him the next morning.

"I hear you've found our negligent groom, sis," he said cheerfully when she tracked him down in the stables.

She frowned, her carefully rehearsed speech already thrown off. "I truly think it's more than that, Rafe. You know me. Who did all the rest of you come to when you wanted information about what was going on in the palace? I always seem to hear things. And how many times did I get them wrong?"

Rafe looked at her and sighed. "It's not that I don't believe you, Dellie. But this isn't our palace. You haven't been here long, and you might be missing subtleties only a Northhelmian would understand. We can't go around accusing people of vague conspiracies because you got a bad feeling."

"We can be on the alert, though! The king and queen could increase the security around the palace, for example."

Rafe looked at her for a silent moment, and she tried to calm down. Getting agitated would only make her seem less credible.

Eventually he shrugged and shook his head. "You overhear something concrete, Dellie, and I'll take it to King Richard and Queen Louise myself. And in the meantime, if I see anything questionable myself, I promise I'll let you know."

Cordelia took a deep breath and tried not to tear up. Rafe's words made all too much sense. But it still hurt that her own brother wouldn't back her up.

Rafe's face softened, and he came forward and put an arm around her. "I'm sorry, Dellie. I wish you could relax and have a good time. I'm getting married in a few weeks, and you've finally escaped Lanover. We should be celebrating."

She gave him a weak smile, and he squeezed her shoulders. "That's the way!"

An awkward throat clearing from the entry to the stable made them both turn around. A rush of nerves overwhelmed Cordelia at the sight of Ferdinand. She'd spent so much time rehearsing her now pointless speech to Rafe that she still hadn't worked out what she was going to say to Ferdy.

"I'm sorry, Your Highnesses, were you waiting for me?"

"Waiting for you? No."

"Should we have been?" Rafe's mild question softened the unintended harshness of Cordelia's reply.

She chewed on the inside of her cheek. Why couldn't she

seem to say the right thing? Frederic or Clarisse would have had the words to convince everyone to take them seriously. And they would have managed to be polite while they were doing it, too.

Ferdinand replied to Rafe, but his eyes lingered on Cordelia. "William asked me to choose a new mount for Princess Cordelia. When I saw you both here, I thought perhaps I'd misunderstood, and you've been waiting to go for a ride right now."

Rafe shook his head. "William is going to make an excellent king—talk about a master of delegation." He strode forward and clapped Ferdinand on the back. "He's lucky to have such a good friend he can rely on."

"Thanks—I think. Or are you calling me a sucker?" Ferdinand's face suggested he was unfazed by this suggestion.

"I wouldn't dare," said Rafe with a grin. "You might conscript me into your squad, and then I'd be in trouble."

Ferdinand laughed. "There's always a spot open for you if you're interested. I'm sure I could whip you into shape in no time."

Rafe put up both hands and began to back away. "I'm sure you could, Ferdy, I'm sure you could."

Cordelia giggled behind her hand. She couldn't conjure up the image of Rafe in the military. Despite his proficiency with most weapons, he had always managed to avoid it at home. Clarisse would say it was because he was too frippery—always laughing and making jokes. But Cordelia suspected he disliked the structure and preferred freedom and independence. He had been the only one of the seven of them to go adventuring, after all.

Rafe's backward steps were taking him slowly out of the barn.

"You know, Rafe, Northhelm is a very practical country," said Ferdinand.

"I've noticed," said Rafe.

"We expect younger children, even of the nobility, to have useful occupations. You'll note that even our heir is in a cavalry squad…"

"An interesting observation, indeed, Ferdy. You alarm me greatly. I think I might go and have a conversation with my bride."

He wheeled around and hurried across the courtyard. Ferdinand chuckled as he watched him go, and then glanced at Cordelia.

"I hope you know I'm only jesting. We wouldn't really conscript him against his will."

"Of course not," Cordelia smiled at him a little shyly, relieved that he seemed to be treating her normally. "But I'm curious to see what he manages to come up with. Knowing Rafe, he'll decide on his preferred occupation, and then charm everyone into believing it was their idea."

Silence settled between them for a moment before Cordelia spoke again. "I like it."

"Like what, Your Highness?"

"That even the royalty and nobility are expected to be useful." Perhaps she wouldn't have spent her childhood feeling so overlooked and inconsequential if she had been given an official role to play in the palace.

Ferdinand smiled. "It's the Northhelmian way. William and Marie both struggle a little with the formality here. It's why Marie likes the Arcadians so much—they're much more easygoing. But I don't think the two of them realize how ingrained it is—even in them. Duty and service above all else."

"Sounds a little dour."

"There's a reason Queen Louise is so beloved. She's warm and soft and loving, nothing like a typical Northhelmian royal." He hesitated and cleared his throat. "I couldn't help but overhear the very end of your conversation. Is that what you were talking to Rafe about? Are you unhappy here in Northhelm?"

"No, no, not at all! I love it here actually. The cobblestones, the snow, the warm fires. It's all so picturesque."

"It is, isn't it?" He paused again. "Did you want to go for a ride? Today is the day the townsfolk traditionally put up Midwinter decorations. I think you would like it."

"Yes, please, that sounds lovely." Cordelia barely refrained from giving a little bounce.

She didn't stop to analyze if the happy bubble of anticipation truly came from Midwinter decorations.

CHAPTER 10

The pretty young mare Ferdinand had chosen for her responded to the lightest of touches. Well-trained, but spirited enough to be interesting. Cordelia couldn't stop smiling.

Ferdinand seemed to share her enthusiasm for horses, and they occupied the trip to the main town square with a discussion about her mare, Butterscotch, and some of the other Lanoverian horses she had ridden. Two grooms and two guards trailed behind them.

When they reached the square, she pulled up and cried out in delight. Large red velvet bows had been tied around the black poles of all the lanterns, and someone had brought in the largest evergreen tree she had ever seen. Children ran around laughing and screaming as several townsfolk placed the final touches on the tree's decorations.

Every branch had been covered in colored glass baubles in gold and red and green. And, interspersed among them, were clear glass baubles containing candles. She could only imagine what it looked like at night with the lanterns and candles blazing.

Most of the buildings surrounding the square had large green wreaths on their doors, many decorated with red velvet bows.

Several of them had also laid green boughs along their windowsills and nestled colored baubles in them.

She clapped her hands and looked across at Ferdinand. The pleasure in his face as he watched her delight made her look down and blush.

Before she could think of anything to say, a cry rang across the courtyard. The children had spotted their arrival. A group of older boys broke off from the rest and rushed over toward them.

"Major, Major!" They swarmed around the horses.

Ferdinand nodded a greeting to them all. "I see your parents have done an excellent job of decorating, as always."

"We helped." One of the young boys thrust out his chest. "I climbed up to put the baubles at the top."

"A fine feat. You'll be ready to join my squad in no time."

The boy looked almost ready to burst at this praise. Cordelia hid a smile behind her hand as Ferdinand addressed each of the boys. She would never have imagined he was so good with children.

"Major," said the oldest one, and Cordelia could tell from the way the rest fell silent that she was about to find out the reason for the enthusiastic greeting. "I went out to the lake this morning, and it's frozen solid."

Cordelia didn't understand the significance of the statement, but from the hope reflected in every small face turned up to them, she could see that everyone else did. At least half of the children held their breath as they waited for the major's answer.

Ferdinand looked over at her with a calculating expression. "Tell me, Princess Cordelia, do you like to skate?"

"Skate?"

"Do you have ice skating in Lanover?"

"Oh!" A picture from one of her childhood storybooks sprang to her mind. Several children gliding across a frozen lake with blades on their shoes. It had looked enchanting. "It doesn't get cold enough for our lakes to freeze over. I've seen pictures of it, though."

"Would you like to try it?"

"Please say yes." The whispered plea was just loud enough to be audible.

A slow smile crept across her face. "Why not?" She looked around at the boys. "As long as you promise not to laugh when I fall over."

"We won't let you fall," said the oldest boy gallantly.

"Excuse me, Major Frog." The small voice came from a tiny girl who had crept up among the boys and was now tugging at one of Ferdinand's stirrups.

Cordelia raised her eyebrows at the unfortunately apt nickname, but Ferdinand ignored it.

One of the boys elbowed the girl. "Rita!"

"Oh, sorry." She looked adorably confused, and Cordelia wanted to slide down and kiss one of the girl's rosy cheeks. But there were enough children around the Lanoverian palace for her to know that such an action would not be appreciated. An affront to the small child's dignity.

"What is it, Rita?" asked Ferdinand, addressing her with the same respect he'd shown the boys.

"Can we come, too?"

"What? No!" cried one of the boys.

"Yeah, boys only," said another.

"Boys!" Ferdinand's sharp reprimand brought instant silence. "The princess is hardly a boy, and you were willing enough to include her."

"That's different," muttered one of the boys under his breath. "She's a grown up."

Cordelia could see Ferdinand fighting to repress a smile at this childish perspective. "The men in my squad are expected to show respect toward all," he said sternly. "Without exception," he added when one of the boys opened his mouth to complain.

He looked around at their mutinous faces, and then grinned. "Although I can understand why you're reluctant to have the girls show you up in front of the princess."

The boys' cries of outrage nearly drowned out a chorus of giggles. Cordelia swung around in her saddle and saw a group of girls had gathered behind them. Clearly Rita wasn't acting alone.

Ferdinand shrugged and spread his arms wide. "If I remember correctly, Lauren won the speed skating contest we held last time and Kara won two times before that."

The oldest boy looked sheepish. "We don't mind if they come, do we boys?"

After a quick exchange of glances, the boys admitted that it would probably be all right to have the girls along.

"All set, then," said Ferdinand. "Everyone get your skates and meet back here as fast as you can. And someone bring some skates for the princess."

"She'll fit into my mother's skates. I'll bring them," called one of the boys over his shoulder as he took off running.

Cordelia blinked, and the whole group had dispersed. "Goodness, that was quick."

"They do love to skate. I hope you'll like it, too."

"I admit I feel a little nervous." She imagined what it must be like to glide across the ice. It seemed worth the risk to her dignity. "I also confess to being a little curious. Why are we escorting a group of children on a skating expedition?"

"Decoration Day is only a half-day holiday. All of their parents will be busy working this afternoon, but the children aren't allowed past the city gates without responsible adult supervision. Apparently, their parents decided I fit that description, so now I'm their favorite victim. They know that if I'm not on shift, I can't resist their pleading."

"That's very kind of you, Major."

He shrugged. "I was a boy who loved to skate once, too."

~

They found the lake outside the city gates, on the fringes of the huge forest that carpeted the whole kingdom north of the capital. A layer of blue-green ice covered the decent sized expanse. Cordelia eyed it uncertainly. It looked bumpier than she had imagined.

The children all began to strap on their skates, and Ferdinand directed Cordelia toward a fallen log where she could sit to put on her own skates. The biggest boy and two of the girls had their skates on fastest, and the three of them rushed straight onto the ice.

Cordelia watched them make a large circle around the edge of the lake, going more slowly than she had been picturing. If that was normal skating speed, she felt a little more confident.

"Are we sure it's safe?" she asked Ferdinand.

"That's what they're checking," he said. "It's why they're going so slowly."

Oh. "You trust them to do that?"

"Of course. They've been coming to this lake every winter since before they could walk. They know how the ice should look and feel."

The three of them stopped, clumped together at the far end of the lake. Ferdinand frowned and began to stride around the edge of the lake toward them, but after a moment they took off skating again, and he returned to Cordelia's side, although his eyes stayed on the children.

With some difficulty, she managed to wrestle the skates onto her feet and stood up, grabbing at Ferdinand's arm when she began to wobble. The three skaters returned and smoothly stepped off the ice and over toward the adults.

"What did you find?" asked Ferdinand.

"There's a patch of dark ice at the far end. It doesn't look safe."

Ferdinand frowned.

"But my da was here yesterday," one of the girls said quickly. "He tested the thickness of the ice at this end. It's frozen deep."

"I don't want to see any of you put at risk," said Ferdinand. "I think it would be best if we go back."

"No, no!" cried the children, crowding around. "We promise we'll stay up this end of the lake."

"Please, Major," said one of the girls who had tested the ice. "None of us want to fall through the ice. We'll stay on this side."

He looked around at all the pleading faces. "Oh, all right. But the first person who goes down the other end, gets everyone sent back home."

A cheer went up, and the children streamed onto the ice. Within moments they were racing each other or skating around in circles and other figures. Several of the girls moved away from the others to do small jumps.

Cordelia watched them, fascinated. Everyone seemed to be having a wonderful time, but she could barely keep her balance standing still. And she wasn't even on the ice yet.

She looked down at Ferdinand's feet. "Hey! Where are your skates?"

"I don't skate. I'm even worse at skating than I am at dancing."

"But you said you used to love it as a boy."

His whole body tensed for the briefest moment, and then he relaxed again and shrugged. "Things change."

Her curiosity pressed her to ask more, but her manners kept her quiet. He clearly didn't want to talk about it. "Who's going to teach me to skate, then?"

Two of the girls heard her question and glided over. "We'll teach you. We won't let you fall."

Before she had time to hesitate, the children had dragged her out onto the ice. The smooth surface made her skates nearly slide out from under her, and she grabbed desperately at the supporting arms on either side.

The girls laughed and began to skate slowly forward, tugging her along with them. Their patience surprised her, as they explained how to move her legs. As her strokes got more confident, they cheered her on, never leaving her side and steadying her whenever she needed it.

Soon enough she struck out on her own. She pushed around the ice in small circles, staying close to the edge and Ferdinand. Every time she swept past him, he waved or called out comments or suggestions.

She couldn't get the smile off her face. The sensation was unlike anything she'd felt before. Was this how the birds felt when they flew through the air? Effortless and weightless. Her ankles hurt a little in the boots, but the sensation was worth the discomfort.

She flew past Ferdinand again, waving and smiling. She wished he could be out on the ice with her. She would feel more confident with his hand in hers. Distracted by her thoughts, she didn't notice a small bump in the ice. One of her skates went off in an unexpected direction, and her arms windmilled around, trying to re-establish her balance.

Despite her frantic arm movements, she couldn't regain control of her feet. Flying out from under her, they dumped her straight onto the ice.

"Ooof." Her bottom landed hard on the frozen water. She groaned, not sure what hurt more—her rear or her pride. Looking up she saw Ferdinand's hand extended out to help her up.

"And now you're a true skater. It wouldn't be a proper first experience if you didn't fall over at least once." His smile took the sting out of her incompetence.

After helping her up, he strode back off the ice, and several children skated forward, offering to help her again. But she waved them away, determined to master it. Within minutes she was back to circling confidently. She decided to try striking further afield.

Pushing off she began to pick up pace. Stretching out her arms she let the air whoosh past her, the thrill increasing along with her speed. She flew faster and faster across the ice.

"Princess! Stop!" She heard Ferdinand's panicked cry at the same time as the texture of the ice under her feet changed. Looking around she realized the color had changed as well—she had skated all the way to the far side of the lake.

She tried to slow, but she was going too fast. Her arms flailed, and panic took over as her feet began to slip.

Several of the children screamed as her skates flew forward, and she once again landed hard on the ice. Only this time, she didn't stop. The ice cracked and gave way, and she dropped through into the freezing water.

CHAPTER 11

*P*ain everywhere. She couldn't think, she couldn't breathe. It felt like when she had dipped her hand into the pond in the palace gardens. Except now the knives were stabbing her entire body.

After the first second of paralyzed shock, she recognized the sensation of sinking. Kicking her legs, she reversed her movement, driving back up toward the surface. Her reaching hands hit ice, and panic washed over her. She couldn't hold her breath much longer.

And then one of her hands found the edge of the ice. Gripping it, she pulled her body to the side, aligning with the hole, and propelled her head up and out of the water.

She gasped a big breath of air and then another and another. She knew she was breathing too fast, but she couldn't stop herself.

Blinking the water out of her eyes, she looked around wildly. It felt as if minutes had passed, but the positions of the others made it evident that it had only been seconds.

"Stop, right now!" Ferdinand's bellow carried all the command and authority of his military training, and several of the children, who had been rushing toward her, froze. "Get down, now." They all dropped to their hands and knees. "Now crawl off the ice—slowly."

The children who were far enough away had already skated onto solid ground. She saw Ferdinand running at full pace along the lake shore. Then her hand slipped, and she sank back down.

The terror-filled memory of her hand hitting the ice flooded over her, and she gave a giant kick that pushed her head back out of the water. Her hands grappled around, less and less responsive to her commands. Finally she managed to re-establish her grip on the edge of the hole.

"Princess, hold on!" Ferdinand's calm and commanding voice soothed her blind terror. He wasn't panicking, so she didn't need to, either.

One of the grooms had stayed with the horses and the children, but the other groom and the two soldiers followed close on Ferdinand's heels. One of the children trailed behind them. He caught up when they reached the shore closest to her and stopped. Unwrapping a long scarf from around his neck, the boy thrust it into Ferdinand's hands.

The major nodded but didn't stop to thank the boy, barking orders to the adults instead.

All four men lowered themselves onto the ice and began to crawl forward in a line, each gripping the ankles of the man in front of him. Ferdinand led the way, the scarf wrapped around one of his hands.

"Just breathe, Princess, we're coming," he said. "Nice and deep now. Slower, if you can."

She gasped in a ragged breath, and then forced herself to wait before taking another.

Ferdinand continued toward her, his human chain behind him, until a loud crack rang across the lake. He froze. Resting on his elbows, he tied the end of the scarf into a loop, tugging on it to secure the knot. Gripping the other end, he threw the loop toward Cordelia.

"Princess, grab the scarf. Loop your arm through it. Both of them if you can."

She reached her free hand out, but the scarf slipped through her fingers.

"Keep calm," said Ferdinand, his own voice level and full of confidence. He pulled the scarf back and threw it again. "You can do it."

And this time she managed to slip her hand through the loop. Once the loop had passed as far as her wrist, she gripped the edge of the ice with that hand and let go with the other one, clumsily using it to push the scarf up toward her shoulder. Then she slid her second hand in, managing to squeeze both arms in past the elbow.

"Excellent. Now try to get your arms up onto the ice. And kick up with your legs. Get your body flat along the top of the water."

Cordelia could feel what little energy she had left draining away. But she fixed her eyes on Ferdinand's and gave one last kick. As she did so, he pulled hard on the scarf and her body slid up and onto the ice.

"That's the way." His tone was soothing now, encouraging. "Don't try to get up, just crawl toward me if you can."

He continued to drag her forward by her arms, and she tried to get her knees under her to help, but her body was no longer cooperating with her mind. The seconds it took for her to cross the ice felt like hours. When Ferdinand reached out and grasped her hands in his, a wash of relief swept over her.

Slowly, starting with the last link in their little chain, the men reversed, the back of the group now pulling them all off the ice. As Cordelia was dragged onto the shore, the distant group of children set up a cheer.

Ferdinand ignored them and started issuing orders again.

"Grey, you and Charlie need to make sure the children get back to their parents safely."

"But, Sir, our orders are to stay with you and the princess."

"Well, I'm giving you new orders. And I don't have time for arguments." He turned to the groom. "You'll need to tie our horses behind yours and get them back to the palace."

"Major?" The groom sounded like he wanted to protest but didn't dare.

"Those are your orders, and we don't have any time to waste. Go!"

All three of them began trotting back toward the children.

"Don't…don't we need the horses to get back to the palace…" Cordelia's teeth were chattering so intensely she could hardly get the words out.

"We're too far from any shelter. You would be exposed to the elements the entire ride. The wind chill alone might kill you. I have another way."

She opened her mouth to try to get out another question, but he cut her off.

"I'm very sorry, Your Highness, but you're going to need to take off your wet dress."

Cordelia stared at him. Her mind felt increasingly fuzzy, but she could have sworn he'd told her to get undressed in the middle of the forest.

"I wouldn't ask if it wasn't absolutely necessary." He took off his jacket and held it toward her, raised like a shield in front of his face. "Quickly now. And then put on this jacket."

Her fumbling fingers wrestled with the sopping fabric until it finally gave way and fell at her feet. The weight dropping from her shoulders gave her nothing but relief. Her underclothes were equally soaked through, of course, but the material was lighter and easier for her small frame to carry. She stepped forward and slipped her arms into the sleeves of Ferdinand's jacket. Once wrapped around her, it cocooned her whole body in delicious dry warmth.

Without pausing to ask her permission, Ferdinand scooped her into his arms and cradled her against his chest. As soon as she was settled, he took off toward the forest at a light jog.

She tried to struggle free, but her body didn't respond to her mental commands. "You can't carry me," she protested. "I'm much too heavy."

"Of course I can," said Ferdinand, matter-of-factly. "And your legs certainly can't do it."

She wanted to protest but knew he was right. She decided that courtesy had been fulfilled, and she could stop fighting. Breathing in his warm, musty scent, she nuzzled into his shoulder and let her mind slip away.

CHAPTER 12

"*P*rincess. Princess!" She could hear his voice calling her and his arms roughly shaking her. "Cordelia!"

She forced her eyes open. His arms still gripped her, and the ground still disappeared beneath his steady gait. But the light had changed.

She blinked. The gray didn't disappear, and the trees of the forest didn't reappear. She blinked again and realized she was looking at the gray of a rock wall. Ferdinand was carrying her through a tunnel.

"You can't sleep, Princess Cordelia," said Ferdinand, worry sounding in his voice for the first time. "You might not wake up. You need to stay with me."

Deep shudders racked her body, but she managed to nod her understanding. "Talk to me. Help me stay awake."

"What would you like to talk about?"

She marveled at the strength of his arms around her and the steadiness of his stride. She might be small, but she was still heavy enough to be a difficult burden for a long journey. But she could hardly tell him she wanted to talk about his muscles. She cast her mind around for another topic.

"Where are we?"

"We're in a tunnel, and I'm going to have to ask you to keep its existence and location a secret."

"I didn't see its location, I missed the opening." The memory that she had fallen asleep, however briefly, produced a thrill of fear.

"The end of the tunnel isn't far from where we were at the lake. The opening is in the palace. It's an ancient escape tunnel for the royal family, in case the capital ever comes under attack. They can get out, all the way past the walls. Only a trusted few know about it, however."

"I won't tell anyone."

"Thank you." He paused. "Hopefully Their Majesties will understand that our need was dire. This tunnel provides a direct route to the palace, and it's sheltered from the wind and the cold."

"They'll understand. I'll insist on it. They won't want trouble with Lanover. They rely on us for a lot of trade, you know." She smiled up at him sleepily.

He bounced her in his arms, jolting her away from the beckoning unconsciousness.

"Stay awake, Princess. Do you have any other questions?"

She tried to think of one. "How come I haven't seen your parents around the palace?"

Held tightly against his chest, she could feel his muscles tighten in response to her question and felt a little guilty. She was taking advantage of the situation to ask him a personal question. He seemed desperate enough to keep her awake to talk about anything. But she didn't feel guilty enough to take her question back. Her curiosity was stronger.

"They live on their estates."

"Don't they ever come to court? Are they coming for the wedding?" It seemed a little strange. A Marquis was an important member of court.

"They'll come for the wedding of course. But they won't arrive until just before Midwinter."

"Why not?"

A short pause gave Cordelia the impression that Ferdinand was attempting to formulate an acceptable answer.

"My family's lands are the second most extensive in the kingdom. Only the Earl of Westforth has greater holdings. My parents have many responsibilities."

The Earl of Westforth. The title sounded familiar. She wanted to let the thought drift away, but no. She was supposed to stay awake. She fought to chase the memory down.

Ah. She remembered. Hanna. Or rather, Lady Westruther. Her fellow attendant. The Earl of Westforth was her father-in-law. So, Hanna had married into an important family.

Cordelia smiled at the memory of the pastries Hanna had brought to their last fitting. They had been delicious. She certainly couldn't think of anyone who seemed more deserving of a high title.

What she really wanted to ask Ferdinand was what had happened to misshape his legs so that he could no longer dance and skate. But even in her confused state, she knew that was a step too far.

"Major," she said, not entirely sure what she planned to say next.

Thankfully he interrupted her. "I think we can get rid of that Major business, don't you? You called me Ferdy once before, and I must say that I rather enjoyed it." Then he rushed on, as if he'd said more than he'd meant to and hoped to cover it up. "Everyone else calls me Ferdy, even your brother. I'm quite used to it."

"All right, Ferdy," she said, as much to stop his flow of words as anything.

He stilled for the briefest moment, his arms tightening around her, and then he picked up his pace.

She tried to remember when she had called him Ferdy before. Oh, of course, the ball. Another memory accompanied it.

"Ferdy, I'm sorry I abandoned you at the ball."

One of his arms jerked slightly.

"There's no need to apologize, Your Highness. You don't need to explain yourself to me."

"But I do. It was horribly rude. I had a very good reason, though. Or I thought I did." She sighed, and her teeth chattered loudly. "When I'm warm again, I'll tell you all about it. I promise."

"Well, don't worry about it for now, Princess Cordelia. We're nearly there. The grooms will have left the children with the soldiers and ridden as fast as they dared through the capital, I'm sure. If we're fortunate, they will have beaten us and they'll be ready for you at the palace. If they tell William or Marie what happened, they'll guess where we've gone. They've skated at the lake many times themselves and know where the tunnel exits."

He cursed so quietly Cordelia hardly caught it.

"What is it?"

"This is all my fault. I shouldn't have let you or the children go skating when they found a thin patch." One of her shudders seemed to pass through into him, rocking them both.

"Don't be ridiculous. It's not your fault." The words felt heavy in Cordelia's mouth. "Obviously it's my fault. None of the children went anywhere near it. I should have been paying more attention to what I was doing. If I hadn't let myself get so caught up in the moment none of this would have happened."

Ferdinand looked down into her face. "You did look so delighted. It was a joy to watch. I just wish I'd called you back sooner. One of the children distracted me, and I lost track of where you were for a moment."

Cordelia tried to form the words in her sluggish mind to reassure him again that it wasn't his fault, but they turned a corner and a bright light made her blink and turn her head into Ferdy's chest.

Voices exclaimed and hands reached out to take her from Ferdy's arms. For the briefest moment she clung to him before remembering how exhausted he must be.

"Thank you," she whispered as new arms swept her away. She hoped he had heard her.

≈

Time passed in a blur. Priscilla and several nurses stripped her down and made her soak in a lukewarm bath. Slowly the shudders eased and then disappeared. Doctors appeared full of questions, and she answered as best she could.

By the end of the day they were predicting a full recovery and declaring her extremely fortunate. "It's a good thing the major was there," said one of them. "He always keeps his head in a crisis. I have no idea how he got you warmed up and back to the palace so quickly, but he managed to do it and that's the important thing."

Over the next few days Priscilla insisted that she stay in her room next to the fire, bundled up against the cold. Cordelia protested a little out of principle but was secretly glad to stay in and rest. Exhaustion still weighted down her movements, an unpleasant reminder of her ordeal.

Rafe visited her every day with some entertaining story to amuse her, and the Duchess of Sessily even stopped by to reassure herself that Cordelia was truly unharmed. The somewhat intimidating woman told Cordelia she was there as a substitute for her mother. Privately Cordelia suspected that her actual mother, who was always as warm as she was calm, would have been a great deal more comforting.

Her only regret was not being able to find Ferdy and thank him again. He had lain on the ice and then carried her for a long distance, all the time without his jacket. She only hoped he hadn't come down sick himself.

Cordelia's mind had, once again, turned to this question when a knock sounded on the door. Priscilla moved to answer it while Cordelia tried to muster some curiosity about her visitor. Unfortunately, the warmth of the flames made her sleepy. She assumed it must be Rafe.

But when the door opened, Marie stood there, a small glazed pot in her hands. She followed Cordelia's surprised gaze to the large red petals of the flowers growing from the pot. The bright color contrasted beautifully with the dark green leaves, an unexpected sight in the middle of the northern winter.

"It's a poinsettia." Marie held it out to Priscilla and gestured for Cordelia to stay in her seat beside the fire. "It's about the only thing that blooms up here in the winter. We keep several pots in the library, and I always borrow one for my room when I'm sick. They're so cheerful." She smiled at Cordelia. "I imagine it's nothing like the flowers you see all year round at home, but it's the best I have."

"Thank you." Cordelia's eyes misted over. Holed up in her room, ill, she had found herself thinking a little longingly of home. The thoughtful gesture from her soon-to-be sister-in-law reminded her that she had family here in Northhelm, too.

Marie sat next to her and filled her in on all the wedding plans and dress fittings she had missed. "Hanna asked after you and said she would bake you something delicious as soon as she has the chance."

"Mmm." Cordelia smiled. Hanna's baking was always welcome. The thoughts of her new Northhelmian friend turned her mind back to Ferdy. "I hope Ferdy is well. I would hate to think he got sick rescuing me."

Marie hesitated.

Cordelia stared at her, all traces of sleepiness gone. "What is it? Is he sick?"

Marie shook her head. "I wasn't sure if I should mention it or not. He's healthy enough, but…"

"Tell me." Cordelia chewed the inside of her cheek, not stopping to ask herself why she felt so distressed at the idea of Ferdy in trouble.

"Some of the nobles aren't happy that he put your life in danger. They've been demanding that my father discipline him in some way. There's talk of taking away his squad and his military rank."

"What?!?" Cordelia sat up straight. "It wasn't Ferdy's fault, it was mine. No one else was injured, were they? Tell the king to send anyone who complains to me, and I'll set them straight."

She fell silent for a moment, frowning. "It's an insult, really. What makes Ferdy responsible for me? Who's to say it wasn't me responsible for him?"

She looked over at Marie and noticed that the other girl looked more amused than incensed. She repressed a sigh. Even here in Northhelm everyone thought of her as young.

Marie picked up her change of mood and reached over to put a reassuring hand on her arm. "You're a guest here, and Ferdy's a Northhelmian. We all share in the responsibility of a host toward you. Your parents have invited Rafe and me to come to Lanover after the wedding, you know. So don't worry, you'll get the chance to be responsible for me."

Cordelia chuckled. "I think I can safely promise you won't be falling through any ice, at least."

"I am sorry that happened." Marie's tone turned earnest. "I'm so glad you're going to be all right."

"It was my own fault. I'd been warned. Please tell that to anyone who asks."

Marie smiled at her. "I'm relieved to hear you say that. Ferdy isn't as charming as William, but he's so dependable that the servants and townsfolk love him. There's been plenty of grumbling on both sides over how this whole situation should be handled."

The sudden clatter of many hooves and the rumble of heavy

carriages made them both turn their heads toward the window. Marie leaped up. "That must be the Rangmerans. I need to get downstairs."

"The Rangmerans?" Cordelia hurried over to the window to peer down into the courtyard. "I thought they weren't arriving until tomorrow."

"Apparently they made excellent time on their journey. A messenger arrived this morning to warn us they would be here a day early."

"Do I need to be there to greet them?"

"Oh no." Marie paused in the doorway. "You'll have the chance to meet them soon enough. This isn't your kingdom, and you're still recovering. Queen Ava will understand I'm sure." She waved goodbye as she said the last words and stepped into the passageway.

"Will she?" Cordelia muttered under her breath, still unsure about the new Rangmeran monarch.

She expected Priscilla to scold her and attempt to call her back to the fire, but instead the older woman followed her over to gaze out the window.

"An impressive entourage. And a smart livery. I approve."

Cordelia bit back a smile—somehow she didn't imagine that the Rangmeran monarchs cared about Priscilla's approval. "I never knew you had such an eye for clothes, Priscilla," she said instead.

"I have spent most of my life in the royal palace, Your Highness. One acquires a sense of such things."

Examining the crowd of servants in the courtyard, Cordelia kept an eye out for the man William believed must be a groom. Surely he wouldn't show himself in the situation.

But, sure enough, there he was. She stared at him intently, ready to raise an alarm if he behaved suspiciously. But the man simply collected a case from one of the carriages and carried it into the palace, one of a long line of servants. He never even went particularly near a horse. Perhaps he wasn't a groom, then.

With the man gone, she turned her attention to the Rangmerans. "There! That must be her." Cordelia pointed to a golden-haired young woman descending from a carriage. The woman turned to speak to a tall man who followed behind her.

"And that must be King Hans."

Cordelia examined the man. She had been expecting a male version of her new friend Hanna, but his hair was chestnut rather than golden. She couldn't see his other features clearly from such a distance, though, so perhaps there were similarities in their features. His bearing proclaimed him as an ex-guard.

She watched him as the other royals came forward to greet the couple, followed by Hanna and her husband, Stefan. He interacted with everyone and greeted his sister with special warmth but, watching from afar, it was clear to Cordelia that he never lost track of Ava. He seemed somehow attuned to his wife in a way Cordelia couldn't explain. Not that Ava looked fragile or in need of his protection. She stood straight and appeared confident as she greeted the rulers of Northhelm, a king and queen old enough to be her parents.

Their dynamic was different from the proud warmth Max displayed toward Alyssa, or the joking friendship between Rafe and Marie, but all three couples seemed to glow with their love. Cordelia had to admit it—William was handsome, charming and kind, but she didn't feel a spark. She didn't miss his company when he was absent or light up in his presence. It would be disappointing to return to Lanover and have to report an entire lack of romance to her sisters.

Turning away from the window, she decided she was finished hiding in her room. If this trip wasn't going to give her romance, it could still give her adventure. Rafe had asked for more evidence, and she had an idea how to get it.

CHAPTER 13

*S*he trod quietly through the palace halls, trying not to draw attention to herself. Her brother hadn't exactly asked her to find more evidence. And he would almost certainly disapprove of her current plan. While he was perfectly willing to face danger himself head on, he didn't approve of the people he loved putting themselves in harm's way. At least, not his younger sisters, anyway.

But Cordelia wasn't a child anymore, and she couldn't trust that she would stumble on another conversation. After all, she already knew the two men had met multiple times without her knowledge. Those had probably been the incriminating conversations, if only she had heard them.

Her adventure at the lake had been unfortunate. But it had also taught her something. Something other than the importance of staying out of ice water, that is. The Northhelmian royal palace had secret passageways. The Lanoverian palace had been sadly lacking in this feature, much to the disappointment of the seven princes and princesses. She smiled. Her parents probably praised their ancestors' forethought in leaving them out. The inevitable childish pranks would have terrorized the entire palace.

But the absence of passageways hadn't stopped the younger Lanoverian royals from searching for them. Celeste had been the scholar among them before the curse, and she had coached them all on how to do it. "Look for something that doesn't fit," she had said. "A row of carvings or patterns where one is slightly different from the others. That could be the mechanism for opening the passageway. Look behind tapestries and knock on the walls. Listen for hollow-sounding spots."

Many merry hours had been spent combing their home for such tell-tale signs.

Searching wasn't as much fun on her own, but the thrill of knowing that at least one passageway definitely existed made up for it. Her memories of arriving in the palace with Ferdy were a little hazy, but she remembered they had come out in the wing that held the royal suites. So she started there, carefully examining the walls with her eyes and, when no one else was in sight, her hands. She didn't want anyone to see her knocking on walls and pulling on carvings.

She had wandered up several corridors and poked through more than one unoccupied sitting room before her knock echoed back to her with a hollow sound. She gave a little jump of excitement. This might be it.

The corridor was constructed from the same smooth stone as the rest of the castle and nothing immediately leaped out at her. She stepped back and carefully assessed the whole space. Not for nothing did her siblings know her as the detailed, observant one.

Two light fixtures bracketed the interesting section of wall, and one of them looked slightly different from the other fixtures she'd seen so far. She couldn't exactly put her finger on what was different—she just knew it didn't look quite right.

Stepping forward, she gripped the metal and pulled it down,

hoping that it wouldn't break off in her hand. That would be hard to explain.

The metal creaked and groaned, and the entire fixture detached from the wall and pivoted down toward her.

"Yes!" she cried as a large section of stone swung away from the rest of the wall. Celine was going to be even more annoyed at being left at home when she heard about this.

Cordelia had lugged a lantern with her on her search, and the effort now paid off. Carefully lighting it, she stepped into the hidden passageway. Celeste had read all about such spaces during their childhood searches and had told Cordelia that the opening mechanisms were easy to find from the inside. So she let the door swing shut behind her without fear.

The narrow passageway was dim but lighter than she had expected. An examination of the walls revealed periodic holes or slits that allowed light to seep into the passage. They must be well hidden from the other side. Cordelia resolved to keep her eye out for them when she left the passageway.

Moving forward, she let her feet lead her without a plan. It quickly became apparent that the palace contained a lot more than a single hidden passageway. The entire building must be riddled with them, a second set of corridors nearly as extensive as the main ones.

Perhaps the original king wanted his servants to come and go out of his sight, she mused. And subsequent rulers had disliked their servants less, so the hidden passages had fallen into disuse. Or perhaps more recent monarchs had simply appreciated their privacy more. The small openings that let in the light also served as spyholes into the rooms and corridors beyond.

Cordelia was relieved that the thick layer of dust indicated no one had been here in a long time. If she hadn't been driven forward by the lingering sense that danger overshadowed them, she would have exited at the first entryway she found. She had no desire to spy on the people of Northhelm.

But somewhere in this palace were the two men she had now overheard three times. If she wanted to overhear anything again, then she needed to find them.

The third hidden entryway she passed removed a lingering doubt from the back of her mind. Celeste had been right; the mechanism for controlling the door was obvious from the inside.

The thick stone muffled the sounds from the main parts of the palace, but Cordelia's excellent hearing allowed her to pick up fragments of conversation here and there. She continued to wander, allowing her vision to blur as she focused on her ears.

There. She stopped and allowed the familiar voice to come into focus. The unknown noble was instructing someone on the items of clothing he wanted prepared for the next day. The soiree to welcome the Rangmerans had been moved forward due to their early arrival, and he wanted to be sure he had an outfit ready.

She shielded her lantern and crept forward as quietly as possible. A little bit of searching revealed a small hole at the right height. Closing one eye, she pressed the other to the opening, hoping she wouldn't find herself looking at a row of books or something.

The room slowly came into focus. The man she had seen at the ball spoke to another man, dressed as a servant. She hadn't seen the second man before. After a few more lines, the noble dismissed him and sat down at an oak desk. He appeared to settle in, writing steadily on a piece of parchment.

Her limited vantage point prevented Cordelia from making out any of the words. After a lengthy period of time passed, she began to feel cramped. Stepping back she stretched, still making an effort to move silently. After a moment's thought, she sat down on the floor of the passageway, ignoring the dust that immediately clung to her dress.

Eventually the man had to stop writing. He would make some

sort of noise when he stood up which would alert her to return to her peep hole.

More time passed, and she began to get bored. She should have brought a book from the small bookcase in her room. Anything would be better than sitting here doing nothing but getting stiff.

At last a noise from the noble's room made her spring to her feet. The same servant who had been discussing the noble's wardrobe had returned to announce the evening meal. He assisted the noble into his jacket and then watched him leave the room. Once the door had swung closed, the servant straightened the room, preparing everything for the noble's return.

After a few minutes, he looked around in satisfaction and followed the noble out the doorway. Cordelia smiled. Unshielding her lantern, she examined the inside of the passageway. She held her breath until she saw the tell-tale outline of a doorway several feet from where she stood.

She wanted to crow with delight but refrained. It was probably better to remain quiet, even if the room was now empty.

Opening the door, she slipped into the room. From the outside, the concealed door looked like a bookshelf. She took out one of the books and propped it open. She didn't want to risk being unable to find the opening mechanism if she needed a quick getaway.

Crossing over to the desk, she saw with disappointment that the parchment had disappeared. The noble had either put it away or taken it with him. She looked around.

It was a smallish sitting room, but a side door opened to a generous-sized bedroom. The whole thing was decorated in heavy red velvet that reminded her of the bows in the town square. Except those had evoked warmth and good cheer while this room seemed ominous and dark. Or maybe her imagination created the difference, fueled by her suspicions about its owner.

The drawers of the desk were locked, so she was forced to

leave them and explore the rest of the room. A fireplace and two small sofas proved entirely uninteresting. She moved on to the bedroom.

Lowering onto her hands and knees, she peered under the bed. Nothing, not even dust. Whoever cleaned this room deserved praise for their attention to detail. Somehow that made her doubt the noble would have left anything out in plain view.

Glancing around with despondency, her eyes caught on something on the dresser. Crossing over she examined the small crystal bottles more closely. There were two, each with a different colored liquid inside. They looked more suited for the dresser of a lady than a man, and the thought reminded her where she had seen them before. The parfumier's stall.

She frowned. She already knew of a connection between the two men from the overheard conversations. But she couldn't determine the significance of her new discovery. Perhaps there was none. Perhaps he had simply bought some scent, for himself or as a gift, alongside whatever other business he was engaged in with the parfumier.

She chewed the inside of her cheek. She needed more information. Nothing in this room would convince Rafe.

Crossing back into the sitting room, she noticed a small card tucked into the edge of a large, gilt mirror. Moving closer she saw that it was an invitation to the royal soiree. The card was addressed to Viscount Ersine.

A sudden noise from the corridor caught her attention. Someone was having a conversation outside the door.

Whirling, she ran toward the open bookcase, reaching down to scoop up the book she had been using as a doorstop. Stuffing it back into its place, she whisked herself through the doorway and pulled it closed behind her, nearly catching her skirts.

It clicked shut just as she heard the main door to the Viscount's rooms open. She clutched her chest as the burst of energy that had shot through her subsided. When she could breathe silently again, she returned to her spyhole and saw the servant had returned with a jug of water and a washbasin.

He disappeared into the bedroom and quickly came back with empty hands. Cordelia shook her head. She had been foolish to assume the man was gone for the night. If he hadn't stopped to speak to someone in the hall, she would have been caught.

She began to move down the passageway, keeping an eye out for a doorway that led into a public corridor or a deserted room. When she found one, she waited until she was sure the coast was clear and then returned to the main palace, taking careful note of how the door looked from the outside.

She now knew the noble's name, but she didn't dare tell Rafe in case he relayed the information to William, and he tipped the man off. Which meant the responsibility fell on her. She would have to ensure she overheard another conversation.

CHAPTER 14

*J*n the following weeks, the weather got even colder, if possible. The palace staff decorated the entire palace with the same green boughs, colored baubles, and red bows she had seen in the square.

William pointed out a sprig of mistletoe that someone had attached above the main doorway to the kitchen, and she saw several servants allowing themselves to be caught by their sweethearts underneath it. Giggles and calls of encouragement always issued from the scullery maids and apprentices in the kitchen when they witnessed the chaste pecks.

"It's not what I expected from Northhelmian formality," Cordelia said to William the first time she witnessed it.

"Ah, but mistletoe is a Midwinter tradition, and tradition is a special form of formality here. You can't go against tradition." He grinned. "An important thing to understand if you're looking to bend the rules. Every system can be played."

After each kiss, a berry was removed from the sprig, but Cordelia noticed that a new sprig, full of berries, appeared every time the old one was emptied. So perhaps the crown prince wasn't the only one in the Northhelmian palace finding ways to bend the rules. She smiled, but it was rather wistful. She wished she had a sweetheart to kiss in the doorway.

Queen Ava turned out to be much more charming than she had envisioned, only occasionally showing a glint of steel behind her pleasant exterior. All the young royals were soon on friendly terms, and the Northhelmians organized an endless number of revelries and entertainments.

Cordelia's intervention had quieted the talk against Ferdinand, and he generally accompanied them. His rank and squad were both still his, but he had been excused from his regular duties with the guard so that he could participate as a member of court during the lead up to the wedding. Cordelia had worried that, with everything that had occurred, their first meeting after her accident might be awkward. But other than clasping her hand tightly and asking after her health, Ferdy acted in his usual manner, and her own discomfort soon eased.

As well as the standard balls and soirees, there were sleigh rides and bonfires and visits to the Midwinter gifts market. They even went ice skating once a team from the palace checked that the lake had completely frozen solid. Cordelia felt relieved, since it seemed like a final exoneration of Ferdinand, but also a little nervous. Ferdy encouraged her to give it another go, however, and Rafe and William took turns staying by her side. The enjoyable memories from her previous experience returned as she whizzed across the ice again.

One cold, clear day, after a particularly heavy snowfall, Ferdinand even led them all into the forest where they built snowmen and rode sleds down a small hill. Cordelia suspected Ferdinand had arranged the excursion after she confessed that she had always wanted to build a snowman, and she feared the activities were a little childish. But, if they were, none of the others seemed to mind, and Rafe instigated a snowball fight that even Hans, the most serious of the group, threw himself into.

After a while, the girls excused themselves and plonked down in the snow to watch the men battle it out.

"Rangmere isn't used to having a ruler who isn't a warrior," said Ava, her eyes lingering on Hans as he caught Max in the back of the head with a large snowball. "I'm actually as competitive as any soldier, though, I just fight differently. In fact, I spend every day fighting against the misconceptions and prejudices around me. And, to be honest, it gets a little exhausting."

She let herself fall backward into the soft cushion of snow. "That's why times like this are so nice. For once what I feel like doing happens to coincide with expectations, and I'm reminded there are some advantages to being an underestimated woman."

Marie looked over at her and raised her eyebrows.

Ava chuckled. "If I were a man I might feel pressured to keep fighting to prove myself." She moved her arms and legs in broad sweeping motions. "But right now, I feel far more like making a snow godmother, so I'm going to leave the fighting to Hans and do exactly what I feel like. When every day feels like an uphill slog, it's good to remember that sometimes expectations work in your favor."

"I know all about not meeting expectations," said Marie, and Alyssa grimaced at her sympathetically. "It never occurred to me to think about the ways in which expectations help me. You have a crafty mind."

"Thank you," said Ava with satisfaction. "A crafty mind is a requirement if you want to rule a kingdom like Rangmere."

"What's a snow godmother?" asked Cordelia. Another reminder that the rest of the royals came from a colder climate, and she didn't quite fit. But they had spent enough time together that she knew she could ask her questions without being laughed at.

Marie offered her hands to Ava who grasped them and allowed the other girl to pull her to her feet. Carefully, she stepped away from the marks she had made in the snow.

"That is a snow godmother."

Cordelia examined the spot where Ava had lain. The sweeping movements of her arms and legs had left behind a shape that looked like a person in a dress with wings.

"Oh, I see." She fell backward and swept her arms up over her head and then back down again, simultaneously pulling her legs together. "Like this?"

"Yes, that's it." Alyssa tipped backward and joined her. "I haven't made one of these in years. I used to make them in the woods around my home when I was a girl and wish that a godmother would come and give me a more exciting life."

"And then one did," said Cordelia, turning her head to smile at her.

"And then one did." Alyssa laughed. "I guess I hadn't thought about it like that before."

Ava had sat back down and resumed watching the snowball fight. "Ferdinand moves surprisingly quickly given his strange gait. I think he's scored at least as many hits as any of the princes."

"He's the eldest son of a Marquis, isn't he?" asked Alyssa, giving Cordelia a sideways glance.

"Yes, the only son," said Marie, also watching the fight. "His legs were straight when we were small children—I don't know what happened to change them, but it doesn't affect him in the saddle, and he's an excellent officer." She shrugged. "I suppose he's found ways of working around it."

Ferdinand popped out from behind a tree and landed a snowball full in William's face.

Ava helped both Cordelia and Alyssa out of their snow godmothers. Admiring her work, Cordelia almost didn't notice that all three girls were staring at her.

"The two of you seem to get along very well," said Alyssa.

Cordelia looked between the three of them and then across at Ferdinand. She blushed. "We're just friends."

"Mmmhmmm," said Ava disbelievingly.

"I don't think of him like that." Cordelia squirmed. She didn't want to admit out loud that his strange looks prevented her from thinking of him as anything other than a friend. It sounded ignoble even in her thoughts, but it was the truth.

"He's a good man," said Marie before letting the matter drop.

The conversation sparked something in Cordelia's mind. Along-side all the entertainment, the royals were using the unique opportunity of being gathered in one place to hold a series of discussions on everything from trade to agriculture. As a junior princess, Cordelia did not attend the meetings, and she had taken to spending those hours, and any others she could find, in the hidden passage next to the Viscount's rooms.

She figured eventually she would hear something.

The boredom of her first visit had inspired her to take her embroidery, so she could work by the light of her lantern. At least it gave her a legitimate activity to show Priscilla when she asked where Cordelia was always disappearing off to.

After all the hours she had spent in the passageway, she now knew how the noble spoke to his servants (imperiously) and how he liked his boots polished (to a mirror shine). But she still didn't have any definitive proof of a conspiracy.

She hadn't even seen any sign of the second man, the one from the parfumier's stall.

She had concluded that she needed another set of eyes. Or, well, ears. She still didn't want to risk Rafe or William finding out the Viscount's title, and Marie was busy planning her wedding.

But she did have another option.

The day after their excursion, she asked Ferdy if he would walk in the gardens with her. He readily accepted, and she gathered her courage and told him the whole story. After the first few lines, a frown appeared on his face and didn't disappear.

"Did you ever find out anything from the head groom? Or about the parfumier?" Cordelia concluded.

Ferdinand narrowed his eyes. "Nothing we could action. But also nothing to contradict your concerns. The parfumier is known as a bit of an unsavory character, but no specific charges against him have been made."

"And the groom?"

"The stable master had no idea which horse I was talking about. He isn't one of the palace ones, and we couldn't find him among the Arcadian animals, either. He simply disappeared."

"Suspicious."

"Very. But there's not much we can do about it. I've put out a request to all the guards to keep an eye out for him, but no one has seen anything yet."

"I don't exactly blame William for not taking me seriously." Cordelia's shoulders slumped. "But I'm horribly afraid I'm right and something terrible is going to happen."

Ferdinand stopped and took one of her hands, holding it tightly between both of his. "Of course I'll help you, Princess Cordelia. It would be an honor as well as my duty."

For the second time, communicating her fears to Ferdinand produced a sensation like a weight falling away.

"Oh good." She smiled at him. "Do you want to see the passageways?"

She had spent a little bit of time exploring the hidden passages, and she now knew the location and secrets of many of the openings. Leading Ferdinand through the palace, she almost skipped with excitement.

Having a friend with her returned some of the initial excitement of her discovery.

"I would never have seen that," said Ferdy, as she showed him the hidden mechanism that opened a door in the wood paneling of an abandoned sitting room.

"That's the idea, of course. But I have an eye for these things." She smiled proudly. It wasn't much, but it was nice to be good at something.

After their conversation, Ferdy disappeared from some of the outings with the royals, and she knew what he was doing instead.

But her favorite hours were when they were both free, and they sat on the dusty floor together. When the Viscount's rooms were empty, they would talk. Cordelia heard all about Ferdy's childhood with William and Marie, and he got the full tale of what it was like to grow up as one of seven royal children.

"When are your parents arriving?" she asked him two days before Midwinter.

The increasing number of dress fittings and other preparations for the wedding had been keeping Cordelia away from the secret passageways despite the underlying tension growing beneath her ribs. Everything was building to a climax and, even with Ferdy's help, she had neither seen nor heard anything conclusive.

She might even have given up on her spying, except that as the palace grew busier, she valued her time hidden away with Ferdy more and more.

"They should arrive by this evening. They'll want to rest before the Midwinter Masquerade tomorrow evening."

"I'm looking forward to meeting them." Cordelia couldn't deny a curiosity to see what they looked like.

"They look nothing like me, thankfully," said Ferdy, filling Cordelia with guilt for being so transparent.

She wanted to protest politely, but it would have seemed a little hollow.

While she tried to think of something to say, a sound from inside the Viscount's room made them both leap up. Positioning themselves at two viewing holes, they saw the noble enter the room. Another man came in behind him.

"Ferdy, that's him," whispered Cordelia, as quietly as she could.

Finally, finally, something interesting was happening.

The Viscount ordered the man to wait and then disappeared into the bedroom. He reappeared carrying one of the small crystal bottles from his dresser.

"Here." He handed it to the man. "Is everything arranged as ordered?"

"Aye." The man took the bottle and slipped it into his rough jacket. "They've brought in extra help for the kitchens, and I've made sure my sister got a place. She'll fetch me once the food has been prepared. It'll be chaos in there, so no one will notice a thing."

"You told her?" The noble sounded angry.

"Of course not. I know my orders. She doesn't know why she's doing it."

The noble frowned but seemed to accept the answer. "There are enough of us in on it already," he muttered, so quietly Cordelia barely caught the words.

"And the queen has issued her usual orders?"

"Aye. All of the royals are to have hot cocoa and mulled wine waiting in their rooms when they return from the ball. My sister will point out the trays, and I'll make sure the poison goes into both types of drink, so we'll be covered whatever they choose."

"Hush," growled the Viscount. "We don't use that word."

The servant went to spit on the ground and then pulled himself up and settled for scowling instead. "I call it like it is."

"Not if you know what's good for you."

The servant narrowed his eyes and then nodded. "Makes no difference to me, Your Lordship, I'm sure."

CHAPTER 15

ordelia stood frozen, too shocked to even turn and look at Ferdy. A mass conspiracy against all the royals. Poison. It was even worse than she had feared.

The servant left and the Viscount stared at the closed door. "This is what happens," he said to the empty room. "This is why we have to act. Elevate one commoner, and they all start to get ideas."

Out of the corner of her eye, she saw that Ferdy was gesturing at her. He picked up the shielded lantern, and led her down the passageway, toward one of the safe exits.

"We have to go to King Richard and Queen Louise immediately."

He led her through the palace so quickly that Cordelia had to trot to keep up. She kept replaying the overheard conversation in her mind. She had a vague feeling that she was missing something obvious, but she couldn't focus enough to work out what it was.

Ferdy led her straight to a meeting room that she hadn't seen before. Two guards kept watch outside the closed door, but one

103

look at the major's face, and they stepped aside. Ferdy strode into the room without hesitating, and Cordelia tumbled in behind him, still trying to catch her breath.

Every head in the room turned toward the intruders. King Richard sat at the head of an oval table of polished wood, the rest of the seats filled by royal representatives from all four kingdoms with their advisors. He looked neither angry nor excited by their interruption.

"Major. This is unexpected."

Ferdy gave a deep bow. "I apologize, Your Majesty, but I have received information that cannot wait."

"The last time someone burst into a boring meeting, it was to announce a rebellion," said Marie from her place next to Rafe. "I hope your news isn't that exciting, Ferdy."

"It isn't good, I'm afraid, Your Highness." Ferdy's expression remained grim, and the smile dropped off Marie's face, too.

Concisely, and without emotion, Ferdy explained where they had been and who they had been watching.

"The secret tunnels?" The king raised a single eyebrow.

"You know the circumstances around Princess Cordelia's discovery of the existence of the passageways," said Ferdy. "I thought she could come to no harm exploring them. No one else has been involved."

The king nodded once, and Ferdy continued their story.

"Poison? Do you know what type?" Alyssa sounded more fascinated than scared. Max put his arm around her shoulders protectively.

"No, Your Highness. Although we have a fair idea where it came from." Ferdy quickly outlined their suspicions about the parfumier and the stallion in the courtyard. "The servant seemed to act alone with the attempted accident and was reprimanded for it. The poison is a more elegant plan."

"It sounds like more people are involved than the two who are known to us," said Ava, who had listened with silent intensity to the reported conversation overheard by Ferdinand and Cordelia. "If we are to discover the rest of the conspirators, we need to understand the motivation for such an action. What do they hope to gain from it?"

"He did say one more thing," said Cordelia, "after the servant left." She glanced at Ferdy.

His lips tightened. "The Viscount seemed to find the servant disrespectful. He said, 'Elevate one commoner, and they all start to get ideas.'"

King Richard looked around the table as everyone present absorbed the words. "Unfortunately, it would appear that you, Princess Alyssa, and you, King Hans, and even you, Marie, are the cause of this outrage. I have been hearing reports for some time now about a small subset of nobles who are offended by the elevation of commoners to royal status. This is the first I have heard of any concrete plan to take action on such feelings, however."

"Is it?" The quiet voice belonged to the Duchess of Sessily. "Or are these the same nobles who pushed for the major to be disciplined for endangering Princess Cordelia?"

The king regarded her for a moment. "You are as astute as ever, Your Grace. It is indeed."

She shook her head. "Their outrage over the sanctity of royal rank and royal persons in that instance seems ironic given the new developments."

Cordelia frowned. "The first time I overheard them, they spoke of a 'madness'. Of 'infected' royals. Perhaps they feel this so-called infection nullifies their royal status." She looked around the room. "One rotten apple and all that."

The duchess regarded her steadily. "It seems we must be grateful for your excellent memory, as well as your diligence in pursuing your suspicions."

King Richard inclined his head. "Indeed, we owe much to Princess Cordelia for her observant eye and ear."

Cordelia flushed and lowered her head, unused to being singled out in such a way. She caught both Rafe and William throwing her guilty looks, apologies on their faces, but the flush of justification she had once imagined failed to appear. She couldn't feel satisfaction for being right when the situation was so serious.

"Excellent, we know who to arrest then," said Hans. His narrowed eyes and balled fists suggested anger. However, Cordelia could see the worry in his gaze whenever it rested on Ava. She had seen enough of him to imagine how he must feel, knowing that their marriage had brought danger to her.

"Certainly we know where to start the investigation," said King Richard. "But we can hardly arrest every noble who has expressed some discontent. It is likely that only a few of them are part of this scheme. Some of them I have known for many years, and I am certain they would not lend their aid to murder, regardless of their opinions on the desecration of rank."

"Yes, indeed, caution is needed," said Alyssa. "The rule of law must be upheld. While I do not doubt the testimony of Ferdinand and Cordelia," she threw them both a smile, "others of the court may not be so convinced."

"A good point," said William thoughtfully. "If we arrest the Viscount without proof, it may only serve to turn more nobles to his cause."

"You have to dare much to win much," said Rafe. "I suggest we do nothing."

"Nothing?" Queen Louise regarded her soon-to-be son-in-law with shock.

"For now," said Rafe.

"Catch them in the act, you mean," said Ava, her eyes narrowed calculatingly.

Alyssa leaned forward. "That might actually work. And the

risk would be minimal." She shuddered. "I, for one, won't be drinking hot cocoa or mulled wine any time soon."

King Richard frowned. "We'll need guards hidden among the workers in the kitchen. This servant doesn't sound particularly loyal to the Viscount. If we can catch him with the poison in hand, I imagine he will be happy enough to implicate everyone else involved in exchange for a lighter sentence. Those he knows about, anyway."

"My men are up to the job," said Ferdy with confidence. "And I can vouch for their loyalty. I can have several stationed in the kitchens and others stationed at the ball, ready to arrest the Viscount as soon as the poisoner starts talking. The parfumier we can pick up as soon as we have his bottle in hand."

"And what will the rest of us be doing?" asked Cordelia, a little relieved that her role in the drama sounded like it was over.

"We will all be dancing at the Masquerade, of course," said Rafe, smiling at her. His eyes had lit up at the proposed action, and she guessed that he wished he were to be stationed with the guards rather than in the ballroom.

Queen Louise must have seen a shadow of fear in the princess' face, because she got up and came around the table to grasp Cordelia's hand in hers. "Don't worry, Cordelia." Her voice was gentle and understanding. "We will all be together and shall help each other to act unconcerned. The Midwinter Masquerade is our most lavish event, and I hope you all may even be able to enjoy yourselves, once the arrests have been made. It is a frightening plot, to be sure," she glanced over at her children, "but I have noticed that help always comes when it's most needed. The High King and the godmothers watch over us and our kingdoms. And it seems on this occasion they saw fit to send you to save us."

Moisture welled up in Cordelia's eyes. She had never imagined herself as the hero in one of the godmother's tales before. The thought was exhilarating.

～

In the end, Cordelia was glad to have masquerade preparations to fill the never-ending hours of the next day. Waiting and pretending that everything was normal proved difficult when every nerve felt as if it were singing and humming. The girls all flitted in and out of each other's rooms, assisting with dress choice and the placement of accessories, and exchanging whispers about the plans for the evening. Everyone from the meeting room had been sworn to secrecy—not even their servants could know what was happening. Thankfully Priscilla assumed that the masquerade and the upcoming wedding were responsible for Cordelia's jitters and didn't ask her to explain herself.

Finally the time arrived for the beginning of the festivities. Cordelia smoothed her purple gown as she made her way toward the ballroom. The tiniest flecks of amethyst had been sewn into the bodice, and the garment sparkled as she moved, the full skirt swishing around her hips. She knew she had never looked so beautiful, but she could take no pleasure in it. More important things were happening tonight.

A steady stream of bright gowns and smart suits entered the ballroom. Unlike at the previous balls, no herald announced the guests. It was a masquerade, after all.

But Cordelia didn't need an announcement to identify Viscount Ersine. She had spent enough hours watching the man to easily recognize him despite the simple black mask that covered his eyes. She shivered. He looked dangerous and deadly.

She lingered at the back of the crowd, reluctant to enter the ballroom. Seeing the Viscount had brought the niggling sense of something forgotten back to her mind.

An indrawn breath made her glance to the side. Ferdy stood there, a look of wonder on his face.

He stepped forward and bowed over her hand. "You look beautiful, Princess Cordelia."

"Thank you, Ferdy." She was too distracted to enjoy the light in his eyes as they rested on her. "I'm so glad you're here. I was wishing someone would show up, and I should have known it would be you." She smiled at him.

"Yes, that's me. Always dependable." He sounded rather depressed about it.

Cordelia ignored him, reaching out to grip his arm. "Did we miss something? I keep feeling like I missed something."

Ferdy lowered his voice. "I don't believe so, Your Highness. All of the guards are in place."

"No, I mean something back at the Viscount's rooms." She frowned, running back over everything she had seen and heard.

She gasped. "The bottles! Ferdy, the bottles!"

"What do you mean?" He looked concerned but confused.

"When I went into the Viscount's rooms, there were two bottles on his dresser, each with a different colored liquid."

"You went into his rooms?" Ferdy sounded thunderous.

She bit her lip and looked up at him a little guiltily. "I might not have mentioned that part."

"That was extremely dangerous, Your Highness!"

She remembered her narrow escape and silently conceded he was right. Outwardly though, she ignored the comment.

"That's not important. What matters is what's in the other bottle and what's happened to it now. Why did he have two types of poison? And why did he only give one to the servant?"

Ferdy frowned and eyed her. "That I can't tell you, Your Highness. Perhaps it was a backup of some sort. It may still be sitting on his dresser."

"We have to go check." She tugged at his sleeve. "Do you know the way to his rooms through the regular corridors? I saw the Viscount go into the masquerade, it will only take me a moment to see if the bottle is still there."

She could almost see Ferdinand's mind working behind his

eyes. Finally he nodded and grasped her hand. "Come on, we need to be quick."

The two ran through the corridors of the palace, occasionally passing a startled servant or a noble running late for the masquerade. They didn't stop until Ferdy pulled them up in front of a solid oak door. Two guards stood nearby in the corridor but Ferdy ignored them.

"Are they your men?" whispered Cordelia.

He nodded. "Just in case Ersine manages to escape the ballroom." He pushed the door open and pulled her through into the Viscount's sitting room.

She took over and led the way into his bedroom. She didn't need more than a single glance at the dresser. It was empty. She rushed over and pulled open each of the drawers, tossing the contents onto the floor. She needed to be sure.

"It's gone."

"So we've missed a piece. There's something else going on here we don't know about."

"This is not good. This is not good." Cordelia began to shake from the rush of energy pouring through her body.

Ferdinand stepped toward her and grasped her hand again. The connection steadied her.

"It's not too late," he said. "We still have time to act."

"The servant!"

"Exactly." Ferdinand sounded grim. "I know where my men were to take him."

Once again he led the way as the two of them raced through the palace. Cordelia's breath was coming in shuddering gasps, but she didn't dare slow down. Ferdy wouldn't leave her, and she didn't want to hold him up. Admittedly her long skirts and dancing slippers didn't help. She gathered the material into her hands so she could move more freely.

Ferdy led them out of a side door and to a small guardhouse

inside the palace walls. Only a couple of men were inside, and they leaped to their feet and saluted Ferdy.

"No sign of them yet, Major," said one, eyeing Cordelia in confusion.

"There's been a new development," said Ferdy, just as the sound of boots reached Cordelia's ears. She spun around and peered out of the window of the guardhouse.

A moment later the rest of them seemed to hear the sound, and one of the guards ran to open the door. Six guards came through, dragging the man Cordelia recognized from the market and the Viscount's room.

"You!" he growled when his eyes fell on her. He spat on the floor.

The guard who gripped the man's handcuffs gave him a small shove. "Watch your manners."

"What's in it for me? Seems I'm in for nothing but trouble already."

"It does seem that way," said Ferdy, stepping forward and speaking in the sternest voice Cordelia had heard him use. "But appearances can be deceiving."

"Oh, they can, can they?" asked the man. But his expression lightened and turned calculating.

"It strikes me," said Ferdy, "that you're just a tool."

The man muttered something inaudible.

"And I'm not interested in a tool. I want the hand that wields it. Tell me everything you know and who gave you your orders, and I'll see less trouble finds you than you're expecting."

The man gave a bark of harsh laughter. "I have no interest in protecting them. I wouldn't have done it at all if they hadn't paid so well. I've got nothing against the royals." He eyed Ferdy. "I hear you're the son of a Marquis. Do I have your word as a noble, you'll help me out if I confess?"

"You have it." Cordelia could tell Ferdy hated the need to bargain with such a man.

MELANIE CELLIER

The servant seemed content with Ferdy's assurance and outlined the plot as they had already heard it. Ferdy signaled to one of his men to go and alert the guards in the ballroom to arrest the Viscount.

"But that's not the end of it," the servant continued.

Cordelia and Ferdy exchanged a glance. This was the part they had run here to hear.

"I didn't trust that Viscount further'n I could throw him. What's to stop him deciding he wants to tie up loose ends once it's all over, eh? So, I did a bit of nosing around of my own. Turns out two other nobles are in it with him." He named the two, and Ferdy gestured for another guard to be off to the ballroom. "And the three of them hatched what you might call a backup plan. They had someone on watch in the kitchens. If any commotion occurred, they were to take a second bottle of a different poison to the ball."

"Why not use the same poison?" asked Ferdy.

"This one isn't as potent, apparently, only kills two out of three." Cordelia stared desperately at Ferdy, but his eyes were fixed on the confessing criminal. Two out of three! Faces flashed before her eyes—Rafe, Marie, William, Alyssa, Max, Ava, Hans— she couldn't bear for even one of them to be hurt.

"Why would he want a less potent poison?" Ferdinand didn't let the dire news shake him out of interrogator mode.

"Well, that's what I wanted to know." The man chuckled. "I'm no fool, and I made them pay me some of the gold up front. Then I headed straight to that perfume maker's stall and used it to buy some information." He snorted. "That idiot will take gold from anyone."

"What did he say?"

"Turns out this second poison has one big redeeming quality. An antidote."

"I see," said Ferdy slowly. "If you were arrested, it means the royals were tipped off to the danger. If one of those nobles wanted to poison them, he would have to offer them something he was eating or drinking himself."

"Exactly." The man spat on the ground again.

Cordelia could readily imagine the scene. "You must try some of this quiche, Your Highness. It's simply delicious." It was the kind of conversation starter many people used to try to strike up a discussion with a royal. And it would be rude to refuse. Even with the specter of poison over their heads, it would seem safe if the noble in question were sharing the food.

Ferdy eyed the man off. "I'm guessing they're not the only ones who wanted insurance."

The man chuckled again. "You're a sharp man, Major. I can see I did the right thing in taking your deal. Turned out my gold was enough for more than information. If you reach into the front of my jacket, you might find something of interest."

Ferdy signaled to his men. A second guard came forward to join the one already holding the man in place. And another then searched the man's pockets. He pulled out a dirty rag and unwrapped something hidden inside it.

"Here you are, Major." He handed over a familiar-looking crystal bottle.

"If this is an antidote," said Ferdy, "then I'm sure you won't mind if I give you some." He watched the servant.

"Right you are, pop it in," said the captive, opening his mouth cooperatively. "You heard me before, I'm done with that Viscount. Three drops per person should do it."

Ferdy carefully dripped three drops into his mouth.

The man neither flinched nor attempted to pull away. Instead he made a face. "Funny tasting stuff." He looked around at all the guards. "The way I heard it, you've got a half hour at most to administer that antidote. And it must be a good twenty minutes since the commotion in the kitchen…"

Ferdy didn't waste time replying to the man. He took off out the door, Cordelia on his heels. As they sped toward the palace, she could hear the man addressing the guards.

"A smart major like that, he'll have the antidote administered in no time. Seems to me you lot should be giving me a medal not locking me up."

She wished she shared his confidence.

CHAPTER 16

"*W*hat's the plan?" She panted out the words as they ran.

"We find all the others and give them the antidote. My men will have arrested the conspirators by now, but we don't know who they got to before that happened. And we don't have time to stop and explain the situation and find out what everyone's eaten and drunk. Everyone gets the antidote."

Cordelia nodded her agreement. It made sense.

"I'll be relying on you here, Princess Cordelia."

"Me?"

"It's a masked ball, remember? You've more than proven your eye for detail, so we need you to use that now to find everyone."

Cordelia gulped. No pressure. Only the lives of most of the royals in the Four Kingdoms hung in the balance.

"I believe in you."

She took courage from Ferdy's words. He had been the one to believe her from the start, and the two of them had made it this far.

They burst into the ballroom, and a flood of light and sound overwhelmed Cordelia. Candles blazed on every side as well as far above in the chandeliers, and an orchestra played as couples spun across the dance floor. Jewels reflected the light and made the ballroom flash with color. Six large trees had been placed around the walls, their boughs decorated with ribbons and baubles and more candles.

It was even more beautiful than Cordelia had imagined, but she had no time to stop and enjoy it. She stood at the top of the stairway and surveyed the moving crowd. She ignored the faces, since they were covered by elaborate masks, many with jewels and feathers. Instead she focused on the height of the dancers and their hair and the way they moved.

She tried to recall the dresses that each of the other girls were wearing. "I'll stay up here, you go to them."

Ferdy nodded his agreement just as she caught sight of Marie and Rafe. Tradition dictated that a Midwinter bridal couple wear white and gold to the Midwinter Masquerade, so they were easy to spot.

"There! It's Marie and Rafe. In the center of the dance floor."

Ferdy took off, shoving through the crowd without apology. He was fully the major in this moment. Driven by single-minded determination, his usual respectful attitude toward the royals and the court had been abandoned.

He reached the couple, but she couldn't hear their conversation over the music and the crowd. She ignored them and kept searching. She found King Richard and Queen Louise in the corner, talking with a couple of their advisors. She wasn't clear if the older couple were targets, but it was better not to take chances.

She glanced back at Ferdy and saw him looking at her for direction. She pointed toward the monarchs, and he began pushing through the dancers again. Marie and Rafe were also making their way through the crowd, heading in her direction.

The music continued but many of the dancers seemed to realize something strange was going on. Couples were stopping in the middle of the dance floor and milling around in confusion. Cordelia tuned them all out and focused on her task.

Ava had worn red and Alyssa green, she was sure of that. She couldn't see Alyssa or Max anywhere, but she finally spotted Ava and Hans next to the buffet tables. Their position made them the most likely victims. Had they just moved there, or had they been there for some time?

She waved Ferdinand in their direction. Watching the couple to make sure they didn't move, she recognized their companions. Hans' sister and her husband, Lord and Lady Westruther.

Her eyes widened. Hanna was another commoner who had married a noble. The heir to the richest title in Northhelm according to Ferdy. They might have been targeted, too.

She picked up her skirts and ran down the stairs. Ferdy had made parting the crowd look easy, but the confused dancers jostled Cordelia on all sides. Putting her head down, she pushed forward, ignoring the elbows and shoulders that caught her in the back and sides.

Finally she broke through in front of the buffet. Ferdinand was tipping three drops into Hans' mouth.

"Hanna! And Stefan!" She pointed at the couple.

Ferdy caught her meaning instantly. "Of course. I should have thought of that."

He turned to the bemused couple. "You'd better have some, too."

From the side of the room, Cordelia could see no more than three layers of people deep. "I couldn't see Alyssa or Max," she said to Ava. "Have you seen them?"

"Not recently."

In her stress Cordelia threw the Rangmeran queen a hard look.

Ava held up her hands. "We've long since resolved our differences, I assure you. I wish neither of them any harm. I truly haven't seen them."

Instant guilt filled Cordelia. Ava had been nothing but kind to her. The fear had put her too much on edge.

"Where could they be? Where could they be?" She stood on her toes and tried to see above the heads of the few couples still dancing. "They must still be here somewhere."

The memory of her first ball in this room popped into her head. "The balcony! Ferdy, the balcony!"

She rushed toward the closest open door and burst out into the cold night air. She could hear the others following her, but she ignored them, scanning the long balcony.

The cold had kept most of the dancers inside, but Alyssa and Max were standing arm in arm at the balustrade, looking out over the dark garden. They looked up at the sound of Cordelia's arrival and hurried over toward her.

"What is it?" asked Max.

"Are you all right, Cordelia? You look sick." Alyssa grasped her arm in concern.

Cordelia shook her head. "It's not me that's sick. There was more poison."

"What?" Max looked at the royals crowding out of the ballroom behind her. "What do you mean? Who?"

Ferdy rushed to Cordelia's side and held out the bottle. A small amount of the liquid remained. "We'll explain after you've had some of this."

Max and Alyssa both accepted the drops, casting each other concerned glances.

"Alyssa felt a little unwell," said Max grimly. "That's why we came outside."

"That was strange tasting." Alyssa wrinkled up her nose. "But I'm already starting to feel better."

"Sounds like we got to you just in time," said Cordelia. She wanted to collapse onto the ground in relief. She settled for stepping away from the others and leaning against the balustrade. When was the last time she had drawn a proper breath?

She let the sound of Ferdy's explanation fade away and focused on the sound of the gentle wind through the tree tops. She tried to calculate how many hours it was until the wedding the next day. She hadn't danced a single dance at the masquerade, but she had already had enough excitement for the evening. She started thinking longingly of her bed.

A noise in the garden caught her attention. She tried to focus on it. Was there someone down there? Without thinking, she stepped down the three shallow steps and into the garden. The noise moved away, and she followed it. Maybe another guest had been poisoned and, like Alyssa, had sought the cool of the night when they began to feel ill.

The lights of the ballroom receded behind her without Cordelia noticing. Her feet were tired, and she hurried a little, hoping to catch the person quickly.

The sounds stopped, and she stepped around a small hedge and into the arms of Viscount Ersine. His arms gripped her hard, and he clapped a hand over her mouth before she could take a breath to scream.

Her mind raced, and her heart raced even faster. How was this possible? The Viscount had been arrested.

"So," he said into her ear. "Spying on me are you, little Princess? Trying to be the hero?"

She shook her head, but he ignored her.

"Well you might be exactly what I need to get out of here. Those princes and that dratted major won't dare to come after me while I have you."

"Cordelia." The cry drifted across the garden and several other voices joined it, echoing her name. The sounds spread out, and she guessed they were looking for her.

She struggled, but the Viscount tightened his grip.

"Now, now, Princess. Don't make me hurt you."

Rage rushed through her. Ersine started dragging her backward, but she could still hear the searchers getting closer. If she could get loose for even a moment...

She took one foot off the ground and drove it back into his shin with all the force she could muster. At the same time, she bit down on the hand covering her mouth.

The Viscount cursed and let her go, stepping back instinctively. She didn't hesitate but took off running toward the sound of the searchers. Ersine cursed again and rushed after her.

She screamed and burst into an open space. In the light of the moonlight, she saw William on one side of the garden and Ferdy on the other. Without stopping to think, she turned away from the prince and ran straight for Ferdy. She catapulted full tilt into his arms, and he closed them around her.

The Viscount, too close on her heels to stop himself, also emerged into the middle of the garden. He tried to turn around, but William grabbed one of his arms roughly. Alerted by Cordelia's scream, Rafe and several guards rushed to assist him.

"You may have evaded the guard earlier," said William, "but you won't get away now, so you might as well submit."

Marie hurried toward Cordelia, but Cordelia ignored both her and the struggle around the Viscount. She was too busy looking wonderingly up into Ferdy's face.

She had thought his strange looks meant she could never see him as more than a friend. But in the moment of her greatest terror, she hadn't even considered running toward the handsome prince. Her heart had known what her head had ignored. Beauty didn't matter. Not her own, not her sisters', and certainly not Ferdy's.

She pictured him riding his stallion, throwing a snowball and sitting beside her in the dim passageway. She was in love with him, and she had been for some time.

He also ignored everyone else, staring down into her face. Could he read the revelation in her eyes?

"You are the most exquisite thing I've ever seen, inside and out, Cordelia. And I will fight for you for as long as it takes."

"You don't have to fight for me, Ferdy," she whispered. "I'm already yours."

Lifting onto her toes, she pressed her lips against his. A bright light flashed out and enveloped the entire garden.

imly Cordelia could hear the others crying out, but she clung to Ferdy. At last the light dimmed, and she could see again.

Except the man she was clinging to had been transformed. His legs were straight and strong, making him taller than before. His bulging eyes were gone, and his features were straight and regular. He was every bit as handsome as William.

She stared at him. She could still see the Ferdy she loved in his features, and his smile still melted her heart, just like it had done the moment before their kiss.

"You did it," he said. "You broke the curse."

"Curse?" William appeared at their side. "What curse?"

Cordelia looked around and saw that the guards had led the Viscount away. William, Rafe, and Marie all stood nearby, gawking at Ferdy. She realized she was still in his arms and blushed.

He sighed. "It isn't a nice story, I'm afraid. Didn't you wonder what happened to my legs when we were children?"

William shrugged. "You came back like that from your estates one winter, and you never mentioned it. I figured you'd had an accident and didn't want to talk about it. As for your face… people look different as they grow. I don't know. I was a child, I didn't give it much thought."

"I wondered," said Marie.

Ferdy looked down at Cordelia. "My father is the Marquis of Montrose. He used to be the richest noble in Northhelm and the most influential. My parents were proud people, and they expected everyone to remember their position and importance. Then the Earl of Westforth married an heiress with extensive estates. He overtook my father in wealth, and my father became bitter about it.

"I remember when I was young, he would talk about the Earl all the time." Ferdy stopped and shook his head. "His obsession with his position was poisoning our family. He started neglecting the people on our estates. I liked Stefan, the Earl's son, but my father always insisted that I be smarter and stronger and better than him at everything. One night he boasted at a party that his son was far more handsome than the Westforth boy."

"How awful for you," said Cordelia softly. He tightened his arms around her.

"That night, a godmother appeared. She challenged my parents on their attitude, but my father would not submit. Not even to a godmother, an emissary of the High King. So she said that he would have to learn some humility. She said he would soon regret the consequences of his actions, and that only true love could break the curse he had brought on our family.

"The next morning I woke up with my legs bent and my face misshapen. I had been my father's greatest source of pride—the future hope of my family. My parents were both heartbroken when they saw that I bore the consequence of their folly. Their attitudes had honestly changed, so they begged the godmother to transform me back. What love could be truer than that of a parent?

"But the godmother said that they had learned their lesson,

but I still had to learn mine. I had never thought of myself as particularly proud, despite my parents' attitudes. But all these years I've wondered if some kernel of pride remained hidden away. But now I realize it was the opposite.

"Their expectations had devoured my confidence. I didn't need to learn to be humble—I needed to learn to see my own worth. To value myself." He pressed a light kiss onto Cordelia's hair. "You taught me that, Cordelia. All this time I've thought that someone like you could never love someone like me. It seemed only fitting that William should have you."

William snorted, but Ferdy ignored him. "And then, tonight, I realized that if I didn't fight for you, I would always regret it. You ran to me, not to William, and I remembered that I was the one who had stood beside you all the way. I decided that I wasn't going to step aside for him or anyone. And then you gave me the greatest gift—true love."

He let go of her and pulled a small velvet-wrapped item from his pocket. A lopsided green bow hung from the package. "It doesn't compare with what you've given me, and I didn't think I would ever have the opportunity to give it to you, but I couldn't stop myself buying you a Midwinter's gift."

He lowered himself onto one knee. "It seems that the godmothers have declared our love to be true in a rather flashy way. I'm not a prince, but I will be a Marquis one day. Will you accept this gift from me?" He looked up at her and smiled, the expression lighting up his face. "And now, if you say yes, I'll be able to dance with you, too—all night if you like."

Cordelia looked from Ferdy to Marie, and the light of excitement in the other girl's eyes confirmed her long ago words from the marketplace. Ferdy wasn't asking Cordelia to accept a gift—he was asking her to accept a lifetime.

She drew him back to his feet and took the present from his hand. "Of course I will. And we'll skate together and dance together and ride together until we're old and gray."

Marie clapped. "I couldn't have asked for a nicer wedding gift than true love for one of my closest friends." She paused for a moment and frowned. "It seems a little harsh of the godmother, though. To curse you for your parents' crimes and then leave you to fight through the curse on your own."

"But maybe she didn't." Cordelia looked excitedly from one to the other. "All this talk of gifts reminds me. My sister sent a golden ball as a gift for you, Marie. She said it came from our godmother, and that it's meant to help you find true love. I had completely forgotten to give it to you, and it's been sitting in my room all this time. Except for the day after I arrived when I took it outside and accidentally dropped it in a pond…"

"…And I came and fished it out for you," said Ferdy, finishing her sentence. He took her back in his arms. "Maybe the godmother was looking out for me after all. And how could I mind that it took her so long? You were worth waiting for."

Cordelia blushed again and then smiled as he swept her into the air and kissed her, hard, while the others laughed and protested.

Midwinter morning dawned bright and clear. The guard reported that all of the conspirators had been rounded up, so the kingdom was free to enjoy the wedding and the holiday.

Marie looked elegant and queenly in her huge white wedding dress, and Cordelia glowed as she followed her down the aisle, her eyes on Ferdy who stood at the front to support Rafe.

The fear and worry were gone and only joy and love remained. She had never experienced a more wonderful Midwinter.

EPILOGUE

"Goodness!" Queen Viktoria sounded as surprised as someone of her relaxed nature ever did.

All five of her family members around the table looked up in interest. She held a letter in her hand, but had ceased reading it and was regarding them with all with a look of laid-back astonishment.

"What does Cordelia have to say, Mother?" asked Prince Frederic. The crown prince had inherited his mother's phlegmatic disposition and sounded more calm than curious.

"She's probably having the most incredible time." Princess Celine sighed and pushed her food around on her plate.

Prince Cassian returned to eating but kept his eyes on his mother, patiently waiting for her to share the news. He looked like a younger replica of his father, King Leonardo, who hadn't stopped eating at all. He knew his wife too well to hold his breath. She would explain herself at her own pace.

Only Princess Celeste remained completely still. Inside she buzzed with questions, but silence and stillness were the safest options when she was around others, and after three years, the posture came instinctively. Her mind raced, however, assessing every possibility.

She'd done her best to warn her sister of the possible danger. Had given her the only tool at her disposal. But still, she'd worried every day since that it might not be enough.

"Apparently there was some sort of plot to dispose of the visiting royals. Poison, if you can believe it." The plump queen shook her head in comfortable horror. "And it seems our Cordelia was involved in discovering and defeating the conspirators."

"Cordelia?" Celine's eyes grew huge. "Uncovering plots?" She moaned. "Somebody tell me why I'm always stuck here in boring Lanover?"

The rest of the family ignored her.

"Good for her," said Frederic.

"And excellent for our position within the Four Kingdoms," said the king. "Hopefully they'll all remember their gratitude next time we need to renegotiate one of our treaties."

"And that's not all," continued the queen, unbothered by the varying reactions of her family. "She's fallen in love with one of the nobles there. She's asking for us to send back our consent to their engagement as soon as possible."

Celeste forgot herself for a moment in her relief and opened her mouth to ask for more information about the attackers and their motivations. Instead she went into a coughing fit. It had been a long time since she had experienced such a bad one, and her eyes watered as she attempted to control the paroxysms.

Desperate to regain her breath, she cast around for something innocuous to say.

"How delightful." She barely managed to squeeze out the words, but the coughs instantly stopped once she had.

Her family all regarded her in astonishment, so she plastered on her brightest smile. "Another wedding! I do hope you'll send your approval at once."

Cassian rolled his eyes and turned away from her to address their mother.

Inside Celeste raged. She would have to wait and hope that someone else in the family asked the right questions. Maybe it would be easier to get her hands on the letter later and read it for herself. Her throat was still raw from the coughing, so she carefully kept the happy smile on her face and devoted her external attention to her meal.

She had honed many skills over the years and would expend any effort to free herself from the endless lie she was forced to live. She would find a way to defeat this curse if it was the last thing she did.

NOTE FROM THE AUTHOR

Read Celeste's story in *The Princess Game: A Reimagining of Sleeping Beauty*. Turn the page for a sneak peek!

Thank you for taking the time to read my book. If you enjoyed it, please spread the word! You could start by leaving a review on Amazon (or Goodreads or Facebook or any other social media site). Your review would be very much appreciated and would make a big difference!

To be kept informed of my new releases, and for free extra content, including an exclusive bonus chapter of my first novel, *The Princess Companion* (Book One of The Four Kingdoms series), please sign up to my mailing list at www.melaniecellier.com. At my website, you'll also find an array of free extra content, including a bonus chapter of *A Midwinter's Wedding* retold from Ferdy's point of view.

PROLOGUE

*P*rince Frederic frowned down at the report the steward had just handed him. He would need to take the news to his father as soon as possible.

"There you are, Frederic!"

He looked up and forced a smile for his younger sister. There was no point worrying Celeste about it, she wouldn't understand anyway. "Have you been looking for me?"

She nodded happily. "All over."

He watched her expectantly, but she just smiled at him. "Did you want something?" He kept his voice gentle. He didn't want to upset her, but the bad news he'd just received made it hard to concentrate.

Her face crinkled in confusion. "I suppose I must have..."

After a moment's awkward silence, which she didn't seem to find awkward at all, she pointed at the report in his hands. "What's that? Something lovely, I hope."

He bit his lip and glanced back down at the report. Once he would have happily gone to his young sister for advice, but that time had long since passed. Now he just wanted to shield her from unnecessary worry.

"Oh!" She clapped her hands, not seeming to notice his hesitation. "Is it another wedding?"

He stared at her. "Wedding?"

"Don't you remember? The last letter for Mother was about Cordelia's engagement. Silly!" She giggled.

He wanted to roll his eyes at the idea of Celeste calling *him* silly, but he stopped himself. It wasn't her fault she'd been cursed, after all. He considered trying to explain to her that the letter about their sister's engagement hadn't been the last letter their mother had received, just the last one she had shown Celeste. Or that he held a report, not a letter. But he decided the effort would strain them both far too much.

He couldn't resist a small joke, however. "Who would be getting married? Cassian, perhaps?" He suppressed a chuckle at the idea of his reserved younger brother in love.

"Cassian? Getting married? Is he really?" Celeste looked excited at the idea, and he groaned.

"No. I spoke in jest. Who would he be marrying?"

"I don't know." She frowned before brightening. "But I didn't know who Cordelia was marrying before her letter, either."

Frederic resisted the urge to massage his aching head. "Yes, but Cordelia has been in Northhelm the entire winter. Cassian lives here, with us."

With each passing year, it became harder to remember that Celeste had once been the brightest of them all. The memory of what had been stolen from her, from their whole family, brought an unusual moment of rage. Once she had challenged him, now she just exasperated him. And he worried that one day he would forget and lose all patience with her.

"It's Cassian's birthday today," said Celeste, apparently ignoring what was too complicated for her to understand.

Frederic stiffened. Cassian's birthday celebration. He'd almost forgotten. A good thing Celeste had come to find him, whatever her original reason had been. He could talk to his father about the report while they ate.

"You're right," he said, taking Celeste's elbow and steering her in the right direction. "And we're going to be late for his birthday meal."

CHAPTER 1

"*T*he latest shipment of medical supplies for the palace doctors never arrived." My brother directed the comment at our father.

I carefully kept my eyes on my plate. So, that had been the news in the report. The one he wouldn't talk to me about. At least I'd managed to get him to Cassian's meal on time.

But another missing delivery? That was...what? The third this month?

King Leonardo frowned at his eldest son and heir. "That's unusual. Does the fault lie on our end or with the merchants?"

I glanced at them both out of the corner of my eye. It wasn't the first shipment to go missing, but apparently it was the first that the steward had reported to my family.

Even I had attributed the first one to natural causes. But the first one had been two months ago, and I had been concerned for some time now. It seemed the steward had a less suspicious nature.

I looked over at Cassian, my second oldest brother. He seemed unperturbed at having his birthday meal disturbed by such a conversation. He hadn't wanted anything extravagant for

135

the day; he never did. Perhaps it still felt strange to him to celebrate without his twin, Clarisse, who had long since married and was living in Rangmere.

"Did the merchants have an excuse?" he asked. "They're usually reliable."

They claim to have delivered the supplies to the palace gate, I thought.

"Apparently, they're claiming they made the delivery," said Frederic. "And they want payment."

I hadn't received a report on this particular incident yet, but I didn't need to. I'd read about four previous ones.

My father sighed. "Lanover may be the wealthiest of the kingdoms, but that doesn't mean we will let ourselves be cheated."

I stiffened. Something strange was definitely going on, but I hadn't been able to trace it to its source yet, and trouble with the merchants was the last thing we needed right now. If my father refused to pay, every traveling merchant caravan in the kingdom might decide to head for the borders as fast as they could go.

I opened my mouth, and then shoved a spoonful of cake in before anyone noticed. I knew better than to try to contribute to the conversation. The curse would never allow it. A splitting headache wouldn't help anything, and I needed to hear my father's decision.

"Blatant disrespect!" barked my uncle. Uncle Horace disapproved of irregularity. "Don't pay them a single coin."

I forgot myself for a moment and snorted, but the sound twisted in my throat and emerged as a giggle. My uncle glared at me.

I rushed to cover up my lapse. "I don't think one coin would be enough." I giggled again, this time intentionally. "The merchants always charge so much for the beautiful material they bring for my dresses."

Everyone stared at me.

"They might get angry if you only paid them one coin." I

smiled around at them all with an innocent expression, hoping they would understand my hint.

A momentary pause ensued, as everyone tried to think of a response. My youngest sister, Celine, rolled her eyes, and returned her attention to her slice of cake. Frederic shook his head slightly and Cassian looked at me pityingly.

After an extended silence, my brothers turned back to my father. I maintained my artless smile, although my teeth clenched behind it. I had clearly been dismissed, the foolish child interrupting the conversation of the adults. The three of them were about to let Uncle Horace's pride precipitate them into a kingdom-wide crisis and, thanks to my curse, I was powerless to stop it.

I knew more about what was going on than any of them, and yet they had all looked embarrassed for me. The poor Sleeping Princess. Foolish Celeste, thinking she could contribute something to the conversation.

I knew it wasn't their fault. I knew it was only because of the curse but, for a moment, anger and frustration overwhelmed my good sense. I opened my mouth to speak and was instantly seized by a coughing fit.

Once again, I had the attention of everyone at the table, with the exception of Celine who seemed far too focused on her plate. I suspected she was plotting something, but I struggled to bring my thoughts into line while the coughs still wracked my body.

I held up my fork, and the curse loosened its grip, allowing me enough air to speak. "A crumb." I smiled weakly, my eyes still watering from the attack.

My father sighed and recommended I have some water. I meekly obeyed, my eye catching on one of the footmen, who had come to clear away the empty dishes. I recognized him immediately. He didn't usually wait on our family meals, but then we didn't usually eat the midday meal together at all. Extra servants had been brought in for the special birthday occasion.

He was one of my agents and a good one, too. If I hadn't known to watch him closely, even I wouldn't have noticed him slip the note into the loose crack of the sideboard, the hiding place where we regularly exchanged messages. My fingers itched to retrieve it, but the curse kept me in my chair. I had already forgotten myself once tonight, and I didn't look forward to the consequences if I slipped up again.

Surely the note held information about the latest missing shipment. Perhaps it even included some new clue. It might contain some piece of evidence that would convince my father not to make a rash move. But it remained hidden away, impossibly out of reach.

Of course, my agent had no idea his spymaster sat so close to him. He believed, like my own family, that I was nothing more than the Sleeping Princess. All thanks to my aunt.

A wave of icy cold crept down from my scalp, although my face remained calm. I had long ago subjugated my external reactions. Stillness and a smile were always the safest postures when a wrong look or word could produce a coughing fit or crippling pain. I assumed the pose instinctively now whenever my mind or emotions threatened to break free of the lie I was forced to live.

And nothing threatened my calm façade like the thought of my absent aunt. Which is why I generally tried to avoid thinking of her. I needed a clear head, not one clouded by hatred.

Unfortunately, it's hard not to hate someone who tried to serve you a death sentence when you were only a few days old.

I took a deep breath. I usually kept my emotions under better control. I had to since I was only truly safe from the curse when I was alone. In public, the more I played along, the more license the curse seemed to give me. These days, I usually uttered foolish statements and gave empty smiles without even thinking about it.

"I suppose we'll have to pay first while we investigate what happened to the supplies," said my father, pulling my attention back to the table. "It's best not to upset the merchants over something that may turn out to be a misunderstanding."

I let out a silent breath of relief as everyone began to get up from the table. Perhaps I didn't give my father enough credit.

Celine rushed over and grabbed my arm. "Come on. I want to show you something."

I let her pull me awkwardly toward the door, giving me the opportunity to bump against the sideboard. With a quick, subtle movement, I retrieved the hidden note and tucked it into my dress. I wanted to slip away alone, so I could read it, but Celine had a firm grip on my arm and whispered that it was about a dress. So I could hardly refuse—everyone knew Princess Celeste loved nothing so much as gowns and fashion.

Read on in *The Princess Game: A Reimagining of Sleeping Beauty*.

Royal Family of Lanover

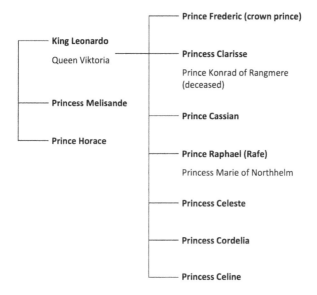

Prince Frederic (crown prince)

King Leonardo
Queen Viktoria

Princess Clarisse

Prince Konrad of Rangmere
(deceased)

Princess Melisande

Prince Cassian

Prince Horace

Prince Raphael (Rafe)

Princess Marie of Northhelm

Princess Celeste

Princess Cordelia

Princess Celine

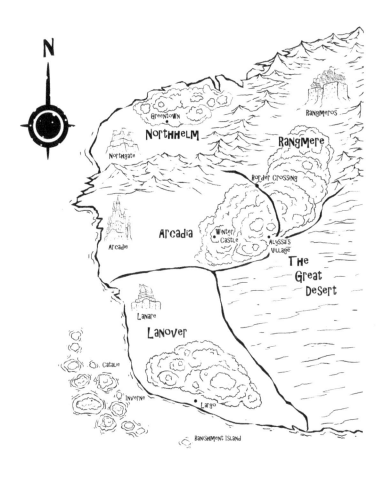

N

Greentown

Rangmeros

NorthHelm

Rangmere

Northgate

Border Crossing

Arcadia

Winter
Castle

Arcadie

Alyssa's
Village

The
Great
Desert

Lanare

Lanover

Catalie

Inverne

Largo

Banishment Island

ACKNOWLEDGMENTS

A Midwinter's Wedding tells the story of a girl from a warm climate who gets to experience a holiday season in the cold north. It's an experience I can relate to since, as an Australian, I'm used to a hot holiday season and no snow at all in most of the country. But I did grow up in the USA and used to love spending our New Year vacation in the snow. I still think fondly of curling up in the warmth with a hot chocolate after spending hours in snowy adventures.

But those years are a long time behind me now, so a big thank you to my northern hemisphere beta reader, Katie, for keeping a special eye on the holiday touches. I had a lot of fun remembering my winter experiences in the US and Europe and imagining what it would be like from Cordelia's perspective.

And, of course, as always, I appreciate all my beta readers more than I can say: Rachel, Priya, and Greg you guys are stand outs, and I am so grateful for your dedication, interest and insight!

Thank you to my cover artist Karri for creating a winter wonderland cover, and to my editors, M.M. Chabot and Dad. I hate to think what this story would look like without your expertise!

And to my family, who walk with me through every difficulty, I'm more grateful than I can say for your support. Don't ever stop being awesome!

And to God, thank you for bringing inspiration in odd moments when I need it the most.

ABOUT THE AUTHOR

 Melanie Cellier grew up on a staple diet of books, books and more books. And although she got older, she never stopped loving children's and young adult novels.

She always wanted to write one herself, but it took three careers and three different continents before she actually managed it.

She now feels incredibly fortunate to spend her time writing from her home in Adelaide, Australia where she keeps an eye out for koalas in her backyard. Her staple diet hasn't changed much, although she's added choc mint Rooibos tea and Chicken Crimpies to the list.

She writes young adult fantasy including her *Spoken Mage* series, and her *Four Kingdoms* and *Beyond the Four Kingdoms* series which are made up of linked stand-alone stories that retell classic fairy tales.

CPSIA information can be obtained
at www.ICGtesting.com
Printed in the USA
LVHW041044280422
717455LV00002B/219